GARFIELD & Co

BASED ON THE ORIGINAL CHARACTERS CREATED BY
JIM DAVIS

PAPERCUTZ ™

NEW YORK

GRAPHIC NOVELS AVAILABLE FROM **PAPERCUTZ**™

GRAPHIC NOVEL #1
"FISH TO FRY"

GRAPHIC NOVEL #2
"THE CURSE OF
THE CAT PEOPLE"

GRAPHIC NOVEL #3
"CATZILLA"

GRAPHIC NOVEL #4
"CAROLING CAPERS"

GRAPHIC NOVEL #5
"A GAME OF CAT
AND MOUSE"

GRAPHIC NOVEL #6
"MOTHER GARFIELD"

COMING SOON:

GRAPHIC NOVEL #7
"HOME FOR THE
HOLIDAYS"

GARFIELD & Co GRAPHIC NOVELS ARE AVAILABLE
AT BOOKSELLERS EVERYWHERE IN HARDCOVER
ONLY FOR $7.99 EACH.

OR ORDER FROM US - PLEASE ADD $4.00 FOR POSTAGE AND
HANDLING FOR THE FIRST BOOK, ADD $1.00 FOR EACH ADDITIONAL
BOOK. PLEASE MAKE CHECK PAYABLE TO: NBM PUBLISHING. SEND
TO: PAPERCUTZ, 160 BROADWAY, SUITE 700, EAST WING, NEW
YORK, NY 10038 (1-800-886-1223)

WWW.PAPERCUTZ.COM

GARFIELD & Co #6 - MOTHER GARFIELD
"THE GARFIELD SHOW" SERIES © 2012- DARGAUD MEDIA.
ALL RIGHTS RESERVED. © PAWS. "GARFIELD" GARFIELD CHARACTERS
™ & © PAWS INC.- ALL RIGHTS RESERVED. THE GARFIELD SHOW- A
DARGAUD MEDIA PRODUCTION. IN ASSOCIATION WITH FRANCE3 WITH
THE PARTICIPATION OF CENTRE NATIONAL DE LA CINÉMETOGRAPHIE
AND THE SUPPORT OF REGION ILE-DE-FRANCE. A SERIES DEVELOPED
BY PHILIPPE VIDAL, ROBERT REA & STEVE BALISSAT. BASED UPON THE
CHARACTERS CREATED BY JIM DAVIS. ORIGINAL STORIES: "MOTHER
GARFIELD" WRITTEN BY MARK EVANIER; "CURSE OF THE WERE-DOG"
WRITTEN BY JULIEN MAGNAT AND JESSICA MENENDEZ; "LITTLE YEL-
LOW RIDING HOOD" WRITTEN BY MARK EVANIER, FROM AN ORIGINAL
IDEA BY PHILIPPE VIDAL.

CEDRIC MICHIELS – COMICS ADAPTATION
JOE JOHNSON – TRANSLATIONS
JIM SALICRUP – DIALOGUE RESTORATION
JANICE CHIANG – LETTERING
JULIE SARTAIN – PRODUCTION
MICHAEL PETRANEK – ASSOCIATE EDITOR
JIM SALICRUP
EDITOR-IN-CHIEF

ISBN: 978-1-59707-318-9

PRINTED IN CHINA
JUNE 2012 BY OG PRINTING PRODUCTIONS, LTD.
UNITS 2 & 3, 5/F, LEMMI CENTRE
50 HOI YUEN ROAD
KWON TONG, KOWLOON

DISTRIBUTED BY MACMILLAN
FIRST PAPERCUTZ PRINTING

ZZZzzzZZz

BANG
SKRISH

CLANG

WHA--?! WAKING ME UP IS A CRIME PUNISHABLE BY NO LESS THAN 15 YEARS IN A MAXIMUM SECURITY PRISON.

GARFIELD & Co
MOTHER GARFIELD

OR AT LEAST, IT SHOULD BE.

ALL RIGHT, I'M UP. LET'S SEE WHO'S TOO STUPID TO NOT BE SLEEPING AT THIS HOUR.

RATTLE KRUN

OH, IT'S YOU, HARRY. WHAT ARE YOU LOOKING FOR?

LEFTOVERS.

IN THIS HOUSE, NOTHING IS LEFT OVER.

SO I SEE.

WHAT I REALLY HAD MY APPETITE SET ON WAS THAT NICE, PLUMP, JUICY BLUEBIRD...

I DOUBT IF YOU'LL FIND A BLUEBIRD IN THERE.

NOW, *THAT'S* WHAT I'M TALKING ABOUT! RIGHT?

I NEVER CHASE ANY BIRD SMALLER THAN A ROAST TURKEY WITH STUFFING, MASHED POTATOES, CRANBERRY SAUCE, AND THAT CREAMED CORN THAT JON'S MOTHER MAKES.

WHAT? GARFIELD ARE YOU SAYING YOU'RE NOT INTO BIRD CHASING?

I GAVE IT UP. TOO MUCH WORK, TOO MANY FEATHERS, AND NOT ENOUGH DRUMSTICKS.

IN THAT CASE, DO YOU MIND...?

CHEEP

BE MY GUEST.

BLUEBIRD PIE, HERE I COME.

OUCH!

CHEEP

YOU WIN THIS ROUND, BIRD. BUT I'LL GET YOU NEXT TIME.

WHAM

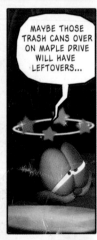

MAYBE THOSE TRASH CANS OVER ON MAPLE DRIVE WILL HAVE LEFTOVERS...

CHASING BIRDS. LOOKS LIKE FUN. BUT I'M NOT GOING TO GET BACK INTO THAT AGAIN. MY CHASING BIRD DAYS ARE BEHIND ME.

NO, NO! THEY'RE AHEAD OF ME! I MUST CHASE BIRDS!

OKAY! IF YOU WERE A CAT, YOU'D UNDERSTAND!

CHEEP

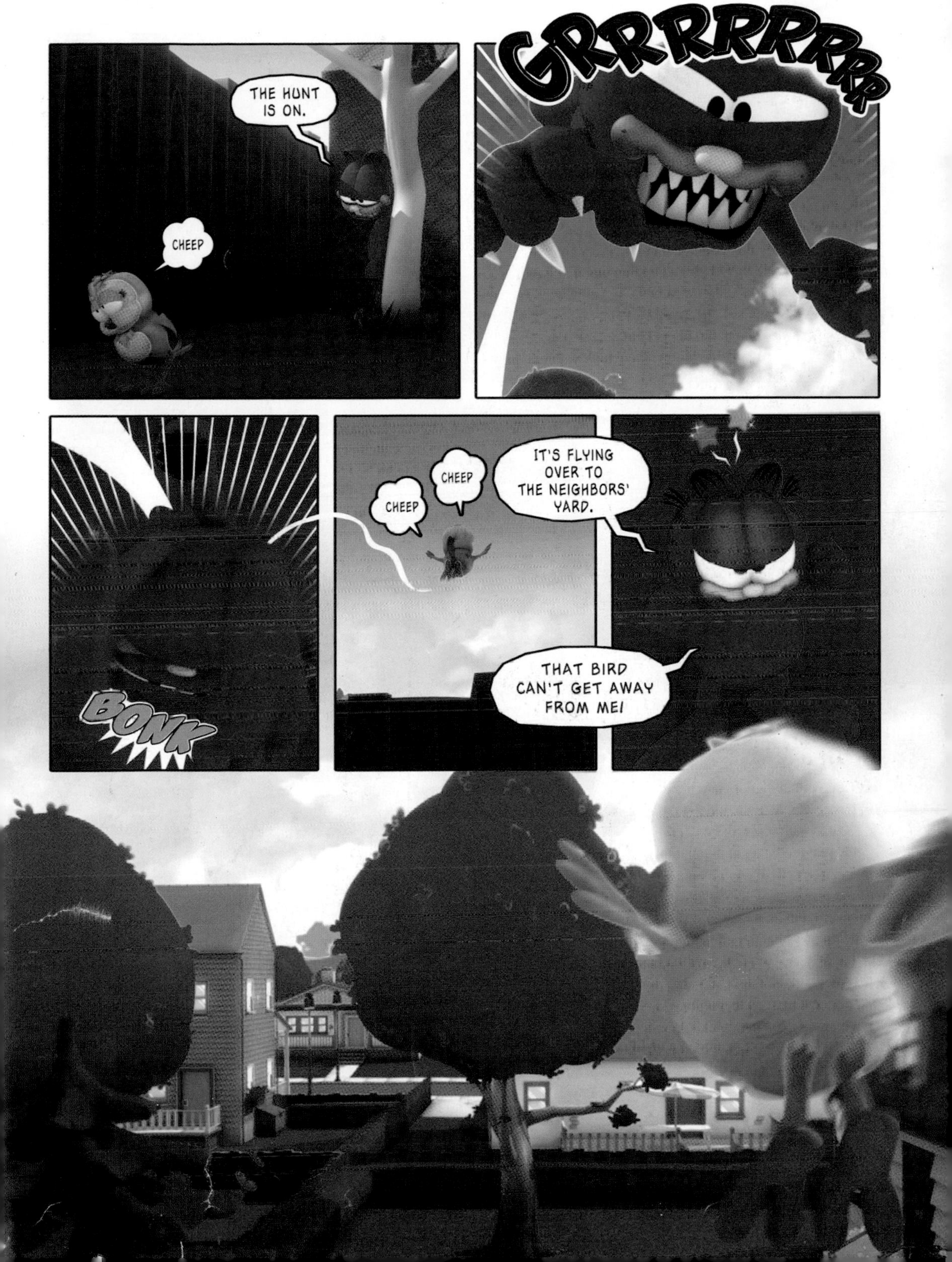
THE HUNT IS ON.
CHEEP
GRRRRRRRRR
BONK
CHEEP
CHEEP
IT'S FLYING OVER TO THE NEIGHBORS' YARD.
THAT BIRD CAN'T GET AWAY FROM ME!

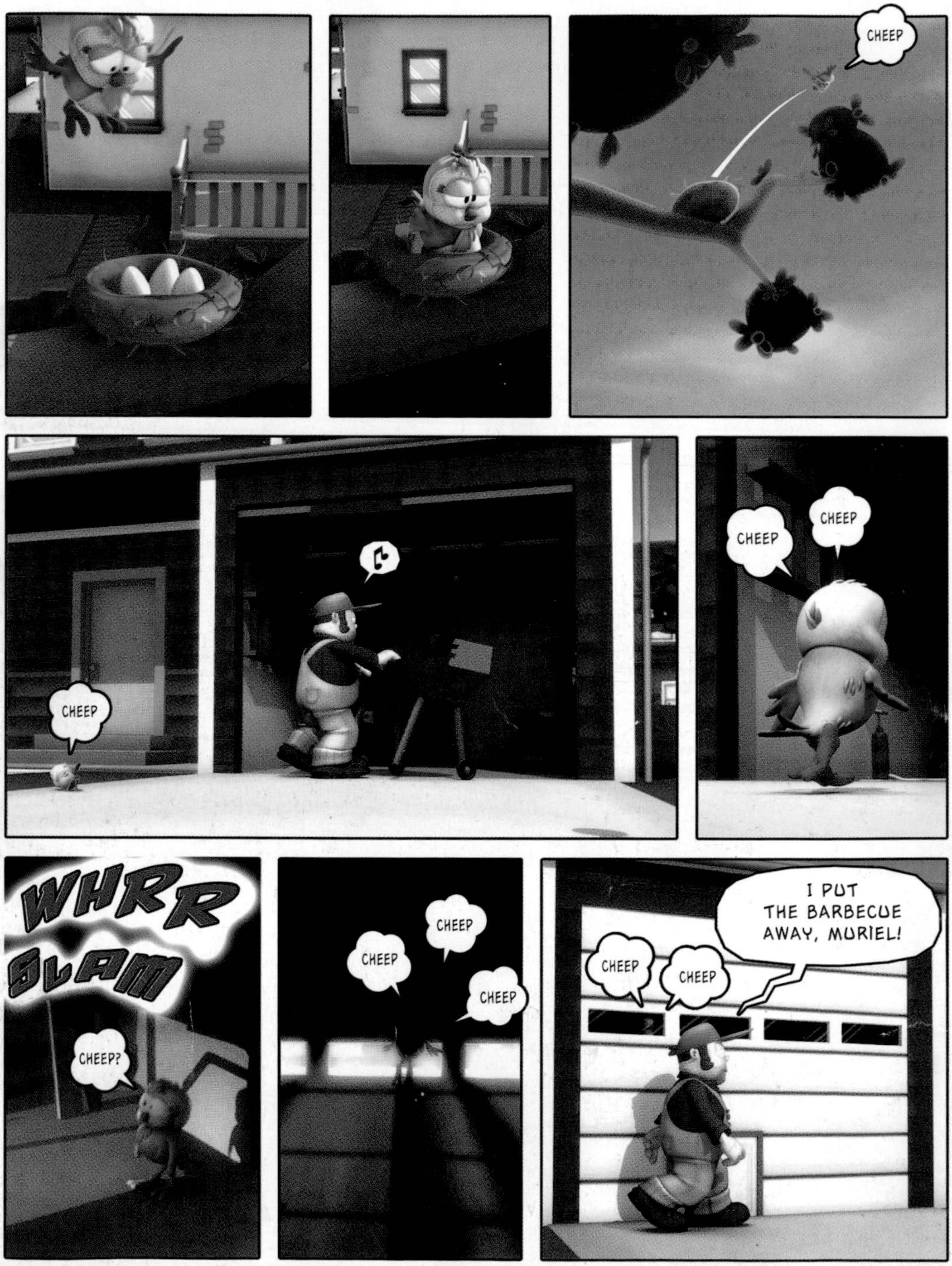
CHEEP
CHEEP
CHEEP
CHEEP
WHRR
SLAM
CHEEP?
CHEEP
CHEEP
CHEEP
CHEEP
CHEEP
I PUT THE BARBECUE AWAY, MURIEL!

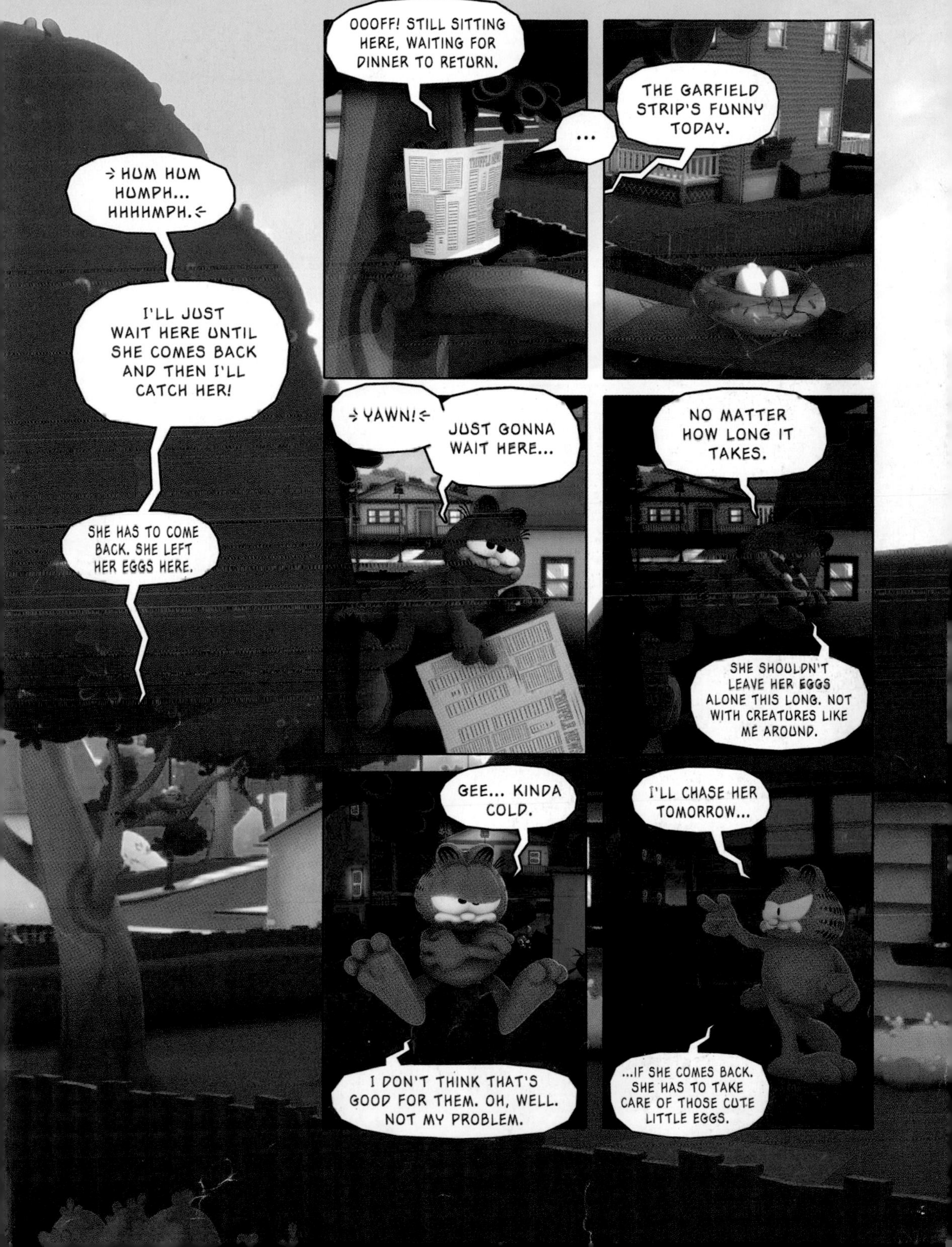
→HUM HUM HUMPH... HHHHMPH.←
I'LL JUST WAIT HERE UNTIL SHE COMES BACK AND THEN I'LL CATCH HER!
SHE HAS TO COME BACK. SHE LEFT HER EGGS HERE.
OOOFF! STILL SITTING HERE, WAITING FOR DINNER TO RETURN.
...
THE GARFIELD STRIP'S FUNNY TODAY.
→YAWN!←
JUST GONNA WAIT HERE...
NO MATTER HOW LONG IT TAKES.
SHE SHOULDN'T LEAVE HER EGGS ALONE THIS LONG. NOT WITH CREATURES LIKE ME AROUND.
GEE... KINDA COLD.
I DON'T THINK THAT'S GOOD FOR THEM. OH, WELL. NOT MY PROBLEM.
I'LL CHASE HER TOMORROW...
...IF SHE COMES BACK. SHE HAS TO TAKE CARE OF THOSE CUTE LITTLE EGGS.

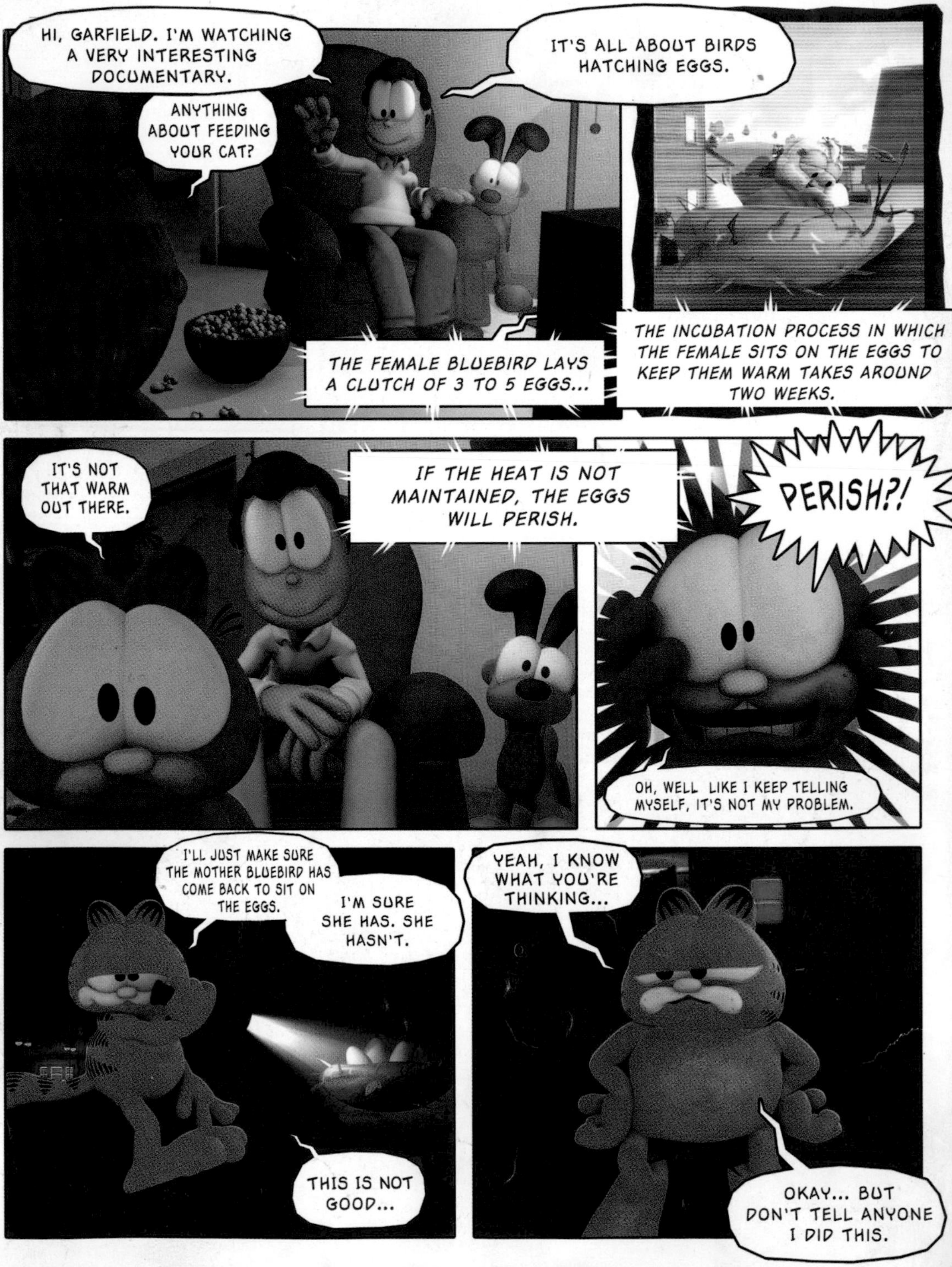
HI, GARFIELD. I'M WATCHING A VERY INTERESTING DOCUMENTARY.
ANYTHING ABOUT FEEDING YOUR CAT?
IT'S ALL ABOUT BIRDS HATCHING EGGS.
THE FEMALE BLUEBIRD LAYS A CLUTCH OF 3 TO 5 EGGS...
THE INCUBATION PROCESS IN WHICH THE FEMALE SITS ON THE EGGS TO KEEP THEM WARM TAKES AROUND TWO WEEKS.
IT'S NOT THAT WARM OUT THERE.
IF THE HEAT IS NOT MAINTAINED, THE EGGS WILL PERISH.
PERISH?!
OH, WELL LIKE I KEEP TELLING MYSELF, IT'S NOT MY PROBLEM.
I'LL JUST MAKE SURE THE MOTHER BLUEBIRD HAS COME BACK TO SIT ON THE EGGS.
I'M SURE SHE HAS. SHE HASN'T.
THIS IS NOT GOOD...
YEAH, I KNOW WHAT YOU'RE THINKING...
OKAY... BUT DON'T TELL ANYONE I DID THIS.

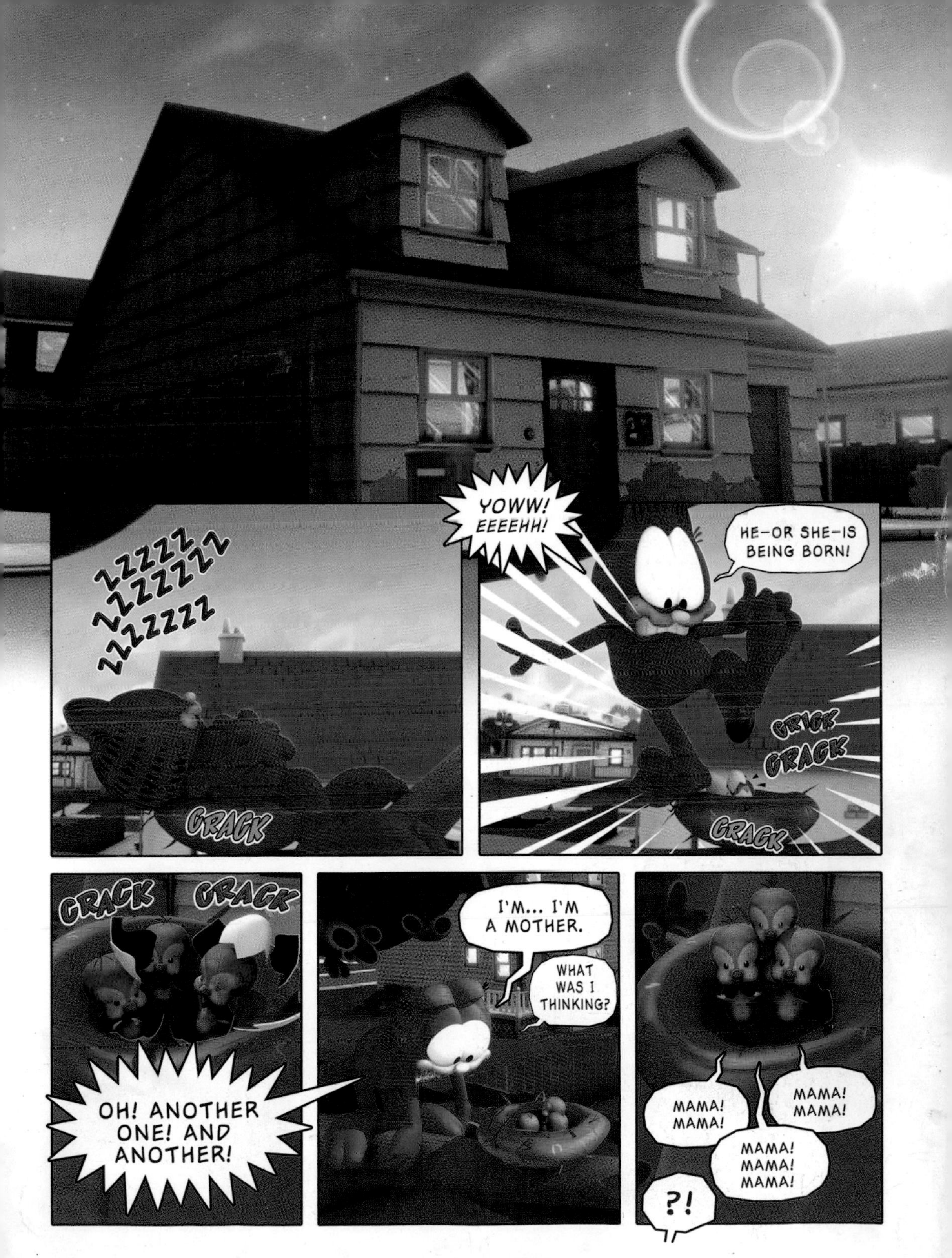
ZZZZZ
ZZZZZZZ
ZZZZZZZ
CRACK
YOWW! EEEEHH!
HE–OR SHE–IS BEING BORN!
CRICK
CRACK
CRACK
CRACK
CRACK
OH! ANOTHER ONE! AND ANOTHER!
I'M... I'M A MOTHER.
WHAT WAS I THINKING?
MAMA! MAMA!
MAMA! MAMA!
MAMA! MAMA! MAMA!
?!

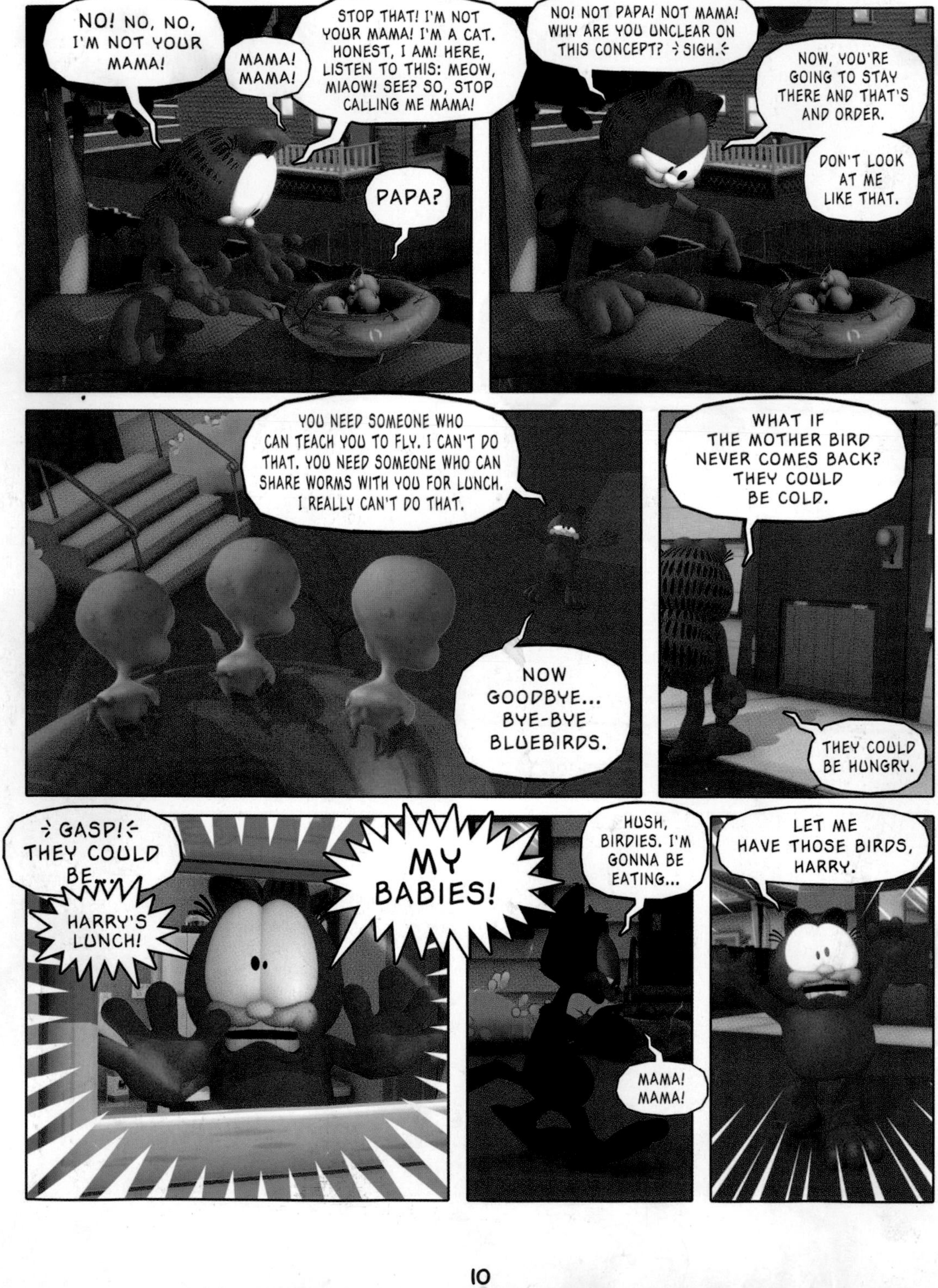
NO! NO, NO, I'M NOT YOUR MAMA!
MAMA! MAMA!
STOP THAT! I'M NOT YOUR MAMA! I'M A CAT. HONEST, I AM! HERE, LISTEN TO THIS: MEOW, MIAOW! SEE? SO, STOP CALLING ME MAMA!
PAPA?
NO! NOT PAPA! NOT MAMA! WHY ARE YOU UNCLEAR ON THIS CONCEPT? SIGH.
NOW, YOU'RE GOING TO STAY THERE AND THAT'S AND ORDER.
DON'T LOOK AT ME LIKE THAT.
YOU NEED SOMEONE WHO CAN TEACH YOU TO FLY. I CAN'T DO THAT. YOU NEED SOMEONE WHO CAN SHARE WORMS WITH YOU FOR LUNCH. I REALLY CAN'T DO THAT.
NOW GOODBYE... BYE-BYE BLUEBIRDS.
WHAT IF THE MOTHER BIRD NEVER COMES BACK? THEY COULD BE COLD.
THEY COULD BE HUNGRY.
GASP! THEY COULD BE...
HARRY'S LUNCH!
MY BABIES!
HUSH, BIRDIES. I'M GONNA BE EATING...
MAMA! MAMA!
LET ME HAVE THOSE BIRDS, HARRY.

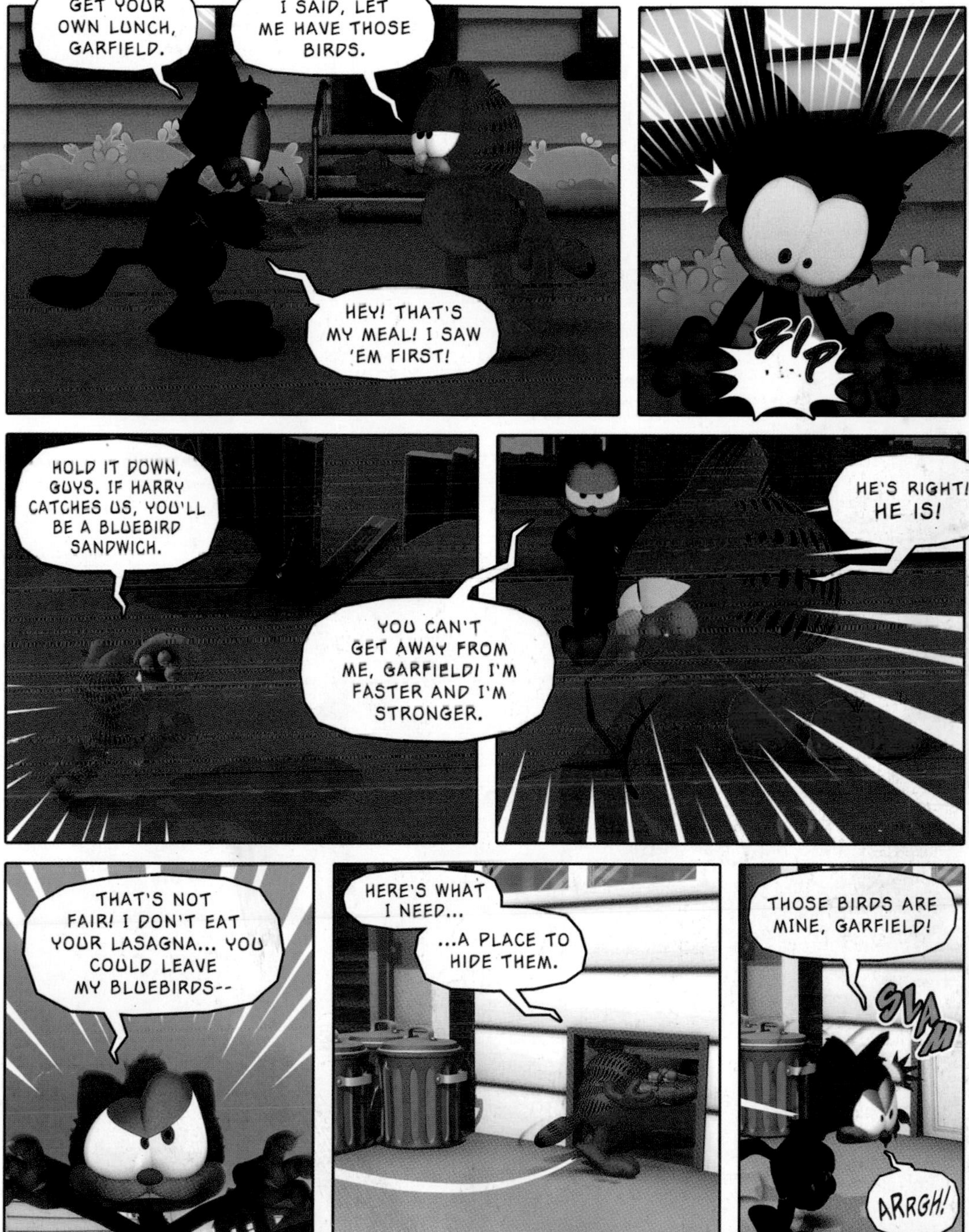
GET YOUR OWN LUNCH, GARFIELD.
I SAID, LET ME HAVE THOSE BIRDS.
HEY! THAT'S MY MEAL! I SAW 'EM FIRST!
ZIP
HOLD IT DOWN, GUYS. IF HARRY CATCHES US, YOU'LL BE A BLUEBIRD SANDWICH.
YOU CAN'T GET AWAY FROM ME, GARFIELD! I'M FASTER AND I'M STRONGER.
HE'S RIGHT! HE IS!
THAT'S NOT FAIR! I DON'T EAT YOUR LASAGNA... YOU COULD LEAVE MY BLUEBIRDS--
HERE'S WHAT I NEED...
...A PLACE TO HIDE THEM.
THOSE BIRDS ARE MINE, GARFIELD!
SLAM
ARRGH!

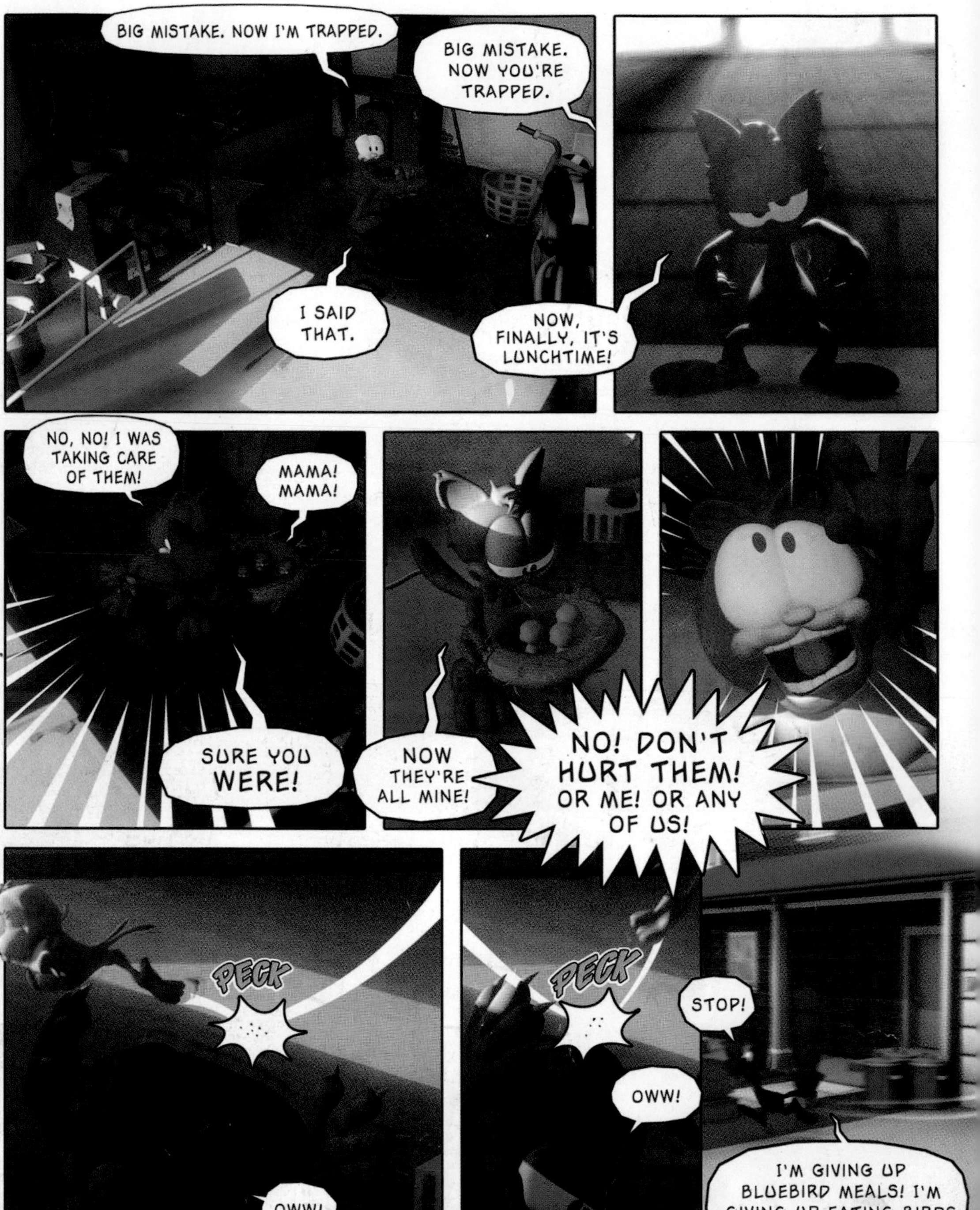
BIG MISTAKE. NOW I'M TRAPPED.
BIG MISTAKE. NOW YOU'RE TRAPPED.
I SAID THAT.
NOW, FINALLY, IT'S LUNCHTIME!
NO, NO! I WAS TAKING CARE OF THEM!
MAMA! MAMA!
SURE YOU WERE!
NOW THEY'RE ALL MINE!
NO! DON'T HURT THEM! OR ME! OR ANY OF US!
PECK
OWW!
PECK
STOP!
OWW!
I'M GIVING UP BLUEBIRD MEALS! I'M GIVING UP EATING BIRDS ALTOGETHER!

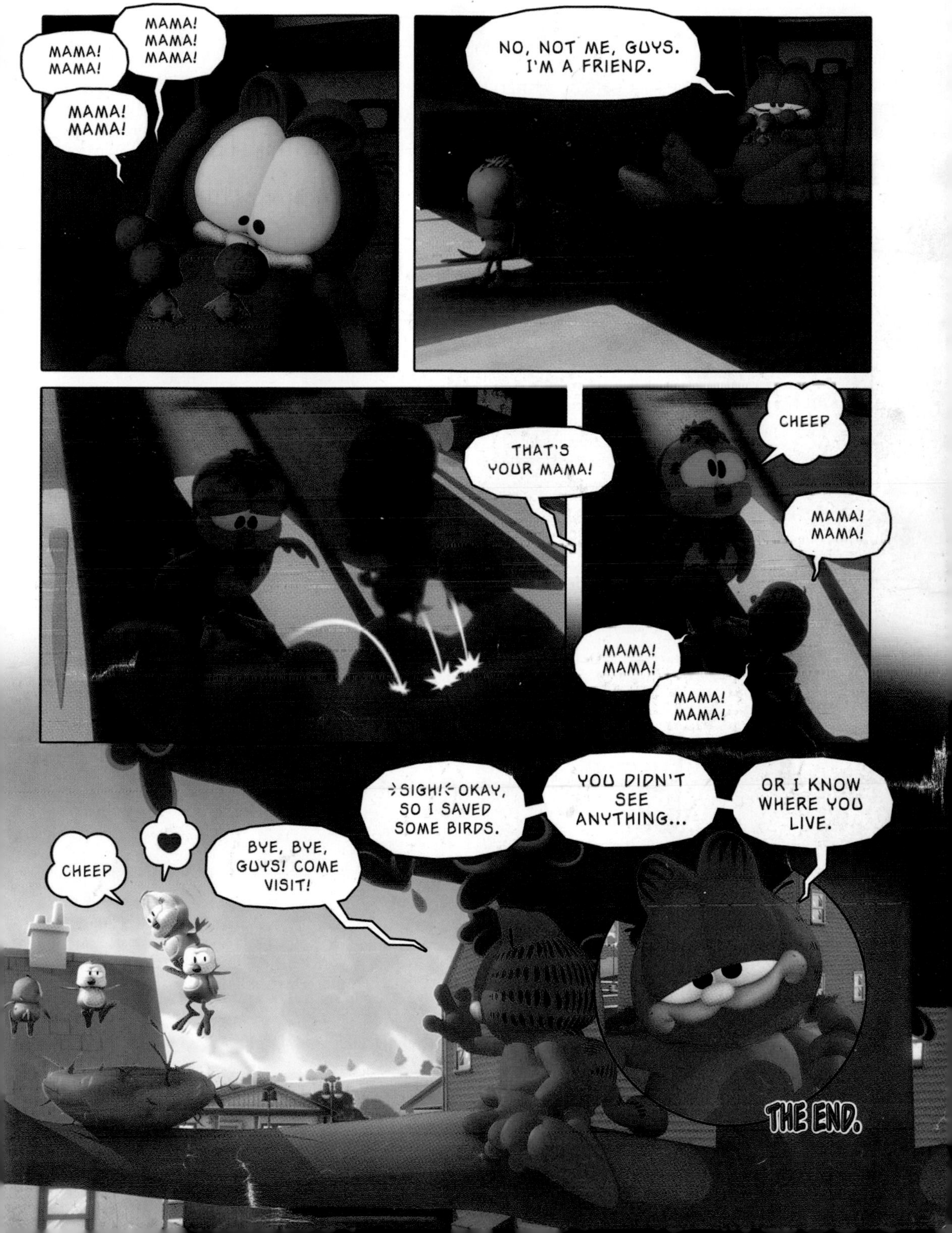
MAMA! MAMA!
MAMA! MAMA! MAMA!
MAMA! MAMA!
NO, NOT ME, GUYS. I'M A FRIEND.
THAT'S YOUR MAMA!
CHEEP
MAMA! MAMA!
MAMA! MAMA!
MAMA! MAMA!
SIGH! OKAY, SO I SAVED SOME BIRDS.
YOU DIDN'T SEE ANYTHING...
OR I KNOW WHERE YOU LIVE.
CHEEP
BYE, BYE, GUYS! COME VISIT!
THE END.

WATCH OUT FOR PAPERCUTZ™

Welcome to the shock-filled sixth GARFIELD & Co graphic novel from Papercutz, the folks dedicated to publishing great graphic novels for all ages. I'm your panic-stricken Editor-in-Chief, Jim Salicrup, warning you that the stories in this graphic novel feature a Garfield unlike any other we've ever seen before!

Case in point: our cover-featured tale showcases Garfield's until-now, well-hidden maternal instincts, when he adopts those three baby bluebirds. That alone would've been more than any true Garfield fan could've ever imagined happening, but it's quickly followed up with a one-two-punch of Garfield actually obeying Jon and not eating an enormous lasagna and a strawberry cheesecake. That something we never thought we'd see—ever.

One has to ask—is this truly Garfield? And the answer, of course, is yes! Just when you thought you knew everything about our favorite lasagna-loving fat cat, stories such as these come along and show different sides to him that we never dreamed existed—but he still remains the same wonderful character that we all fell in love with originally, either on the GARFIELD & Co animated series seen on the Cartoon Network, or in the great Jim Davis comic strips.

Just as Garfield ultimately remains true to himself, I, too, must be me, and mention that as part of this year's FREE COMIC BOOK DAY Papercutz is publishing an extra-special FREE COMIC BOOK DAY comic.

It looks exactly like this (only much bigger!):

FREE COMIC BOOK DAY
the SMURFS
Peyo
PLUS: DISNEY FAIRIES DANCE CLASS AND ERNEST & REBECCA
PAPERCUTZ

And if you flip it, it looks like this:

FREE COMIC BOOK DAY
Disney FAIRIES
TinkerBell
PLUS: THE SMURFS, DANCE CLASS, AND ERNEST & REBECCA
PAPERCUTZ

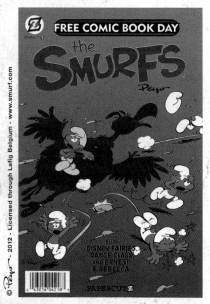

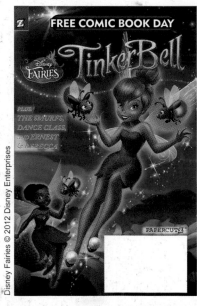

On the first Saturday in the month of May, comicbook shops all across North America celebrate FREE COMIC BOOK DAY by giving away special comics created by many of the top comicbook publishers. Last year, Papercutz published its first FREE COMIC BOOK DAY comic featuring GERONIMO STILTON and THE SMURFS. This year, we featured THE SMURFS, DISNEY FAIRIES, DANCLE CLASS, and REBECCA & ERNEST. So, if you love our GARFIELD & Co graphic novels, here's a fun way to sample four other Papercutz graphic novel series for free! For the location of the comicbook store nearest you, just call 1-888-COMICBOOK.

A quick trivia question—years ago, in an animated TV special, Garfield appeared with some of the characters featured in this year's FREE COMIC BOOK DAY comic. Which characters? Answer at bottom of this page.

All this talk about FREE COMIC BOOK DAY reminds us that our very next graphic novel will also be about a very special day where folks get stuff for free. Don't miss GARFIELD & Co #7 "Home for the Holidays"!We'll be putting a lasagna out in the window for you!

ANSWER: Garfield and the Smurfs, along with many other cartoon characters, all appeared in "Cartoon All-Stars to the Rescue."

Jim

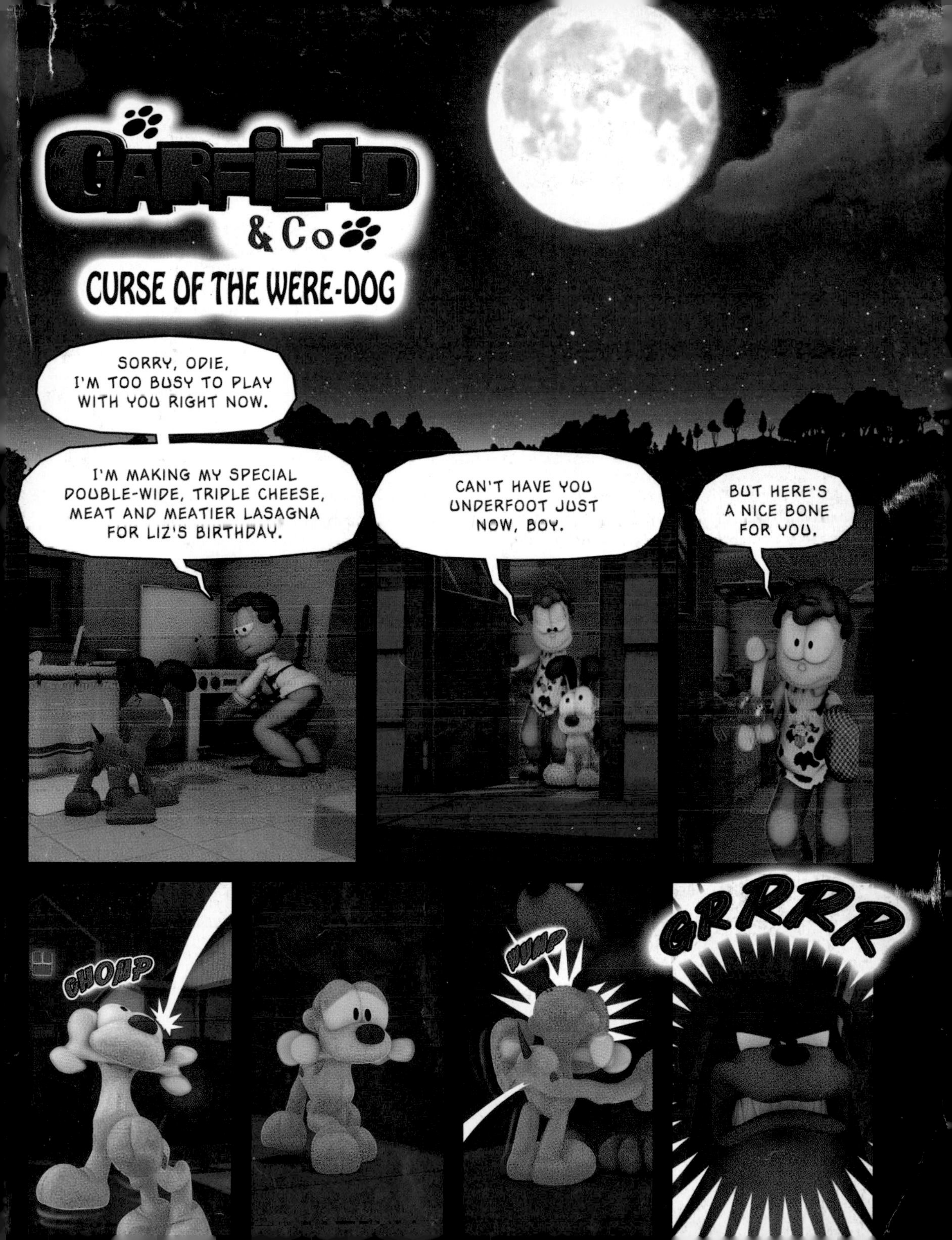
GARFIELD
& Co
CURSE OF THE WERE-DOG
SORRY, ODIE, I'M TOO BUSY TO PLAY WITH YOU RIGHT NOW.
I'M MAKING MY SPECIAL DOUBLE-WIDE, TRIPLE CHEESE, MEAT AND MEATIER LASAGNA FOR LIZ'S BIRTHDAY.
CAN'T HAVE YOU UNDERFOOT JUST NOW, BOY.
BUT HERE'S A NICE BONE FOR YOU.
CHOMP
GRRRR

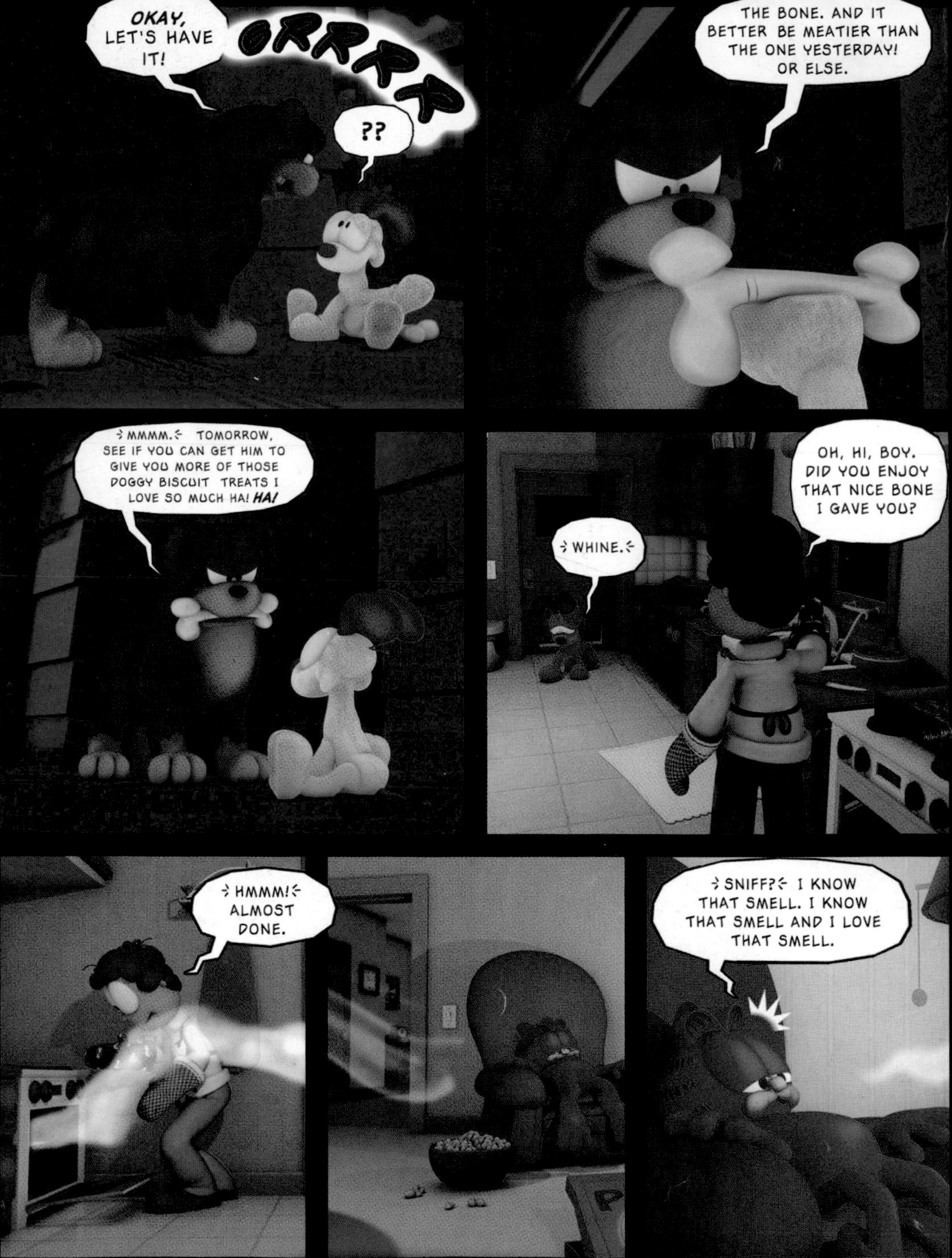
OKAY, LET'S HAVE IT!
GRRRR
??
THE BONE. AND IT BETTER BE MEATIER THAN THE ONE YESTERDAY! OR ELSE.
MMMM. TOMORROW, SEE IF YOU CAN GET HIM TO GIVE YOU MORE OF THOSE DOGGY BISCUIT TREATS I LOVE SO MUCH HA! HA!
WHINE.
OH, HI, BOY. DID YOU ENJOY THAT NICE BONE I GAVE YOU?
HMMM! ALMOST DONE.
SNIFF? I KNOW THAT SMELL. I KNOW THAT SMELL AND I LOVE THAT SMELL.

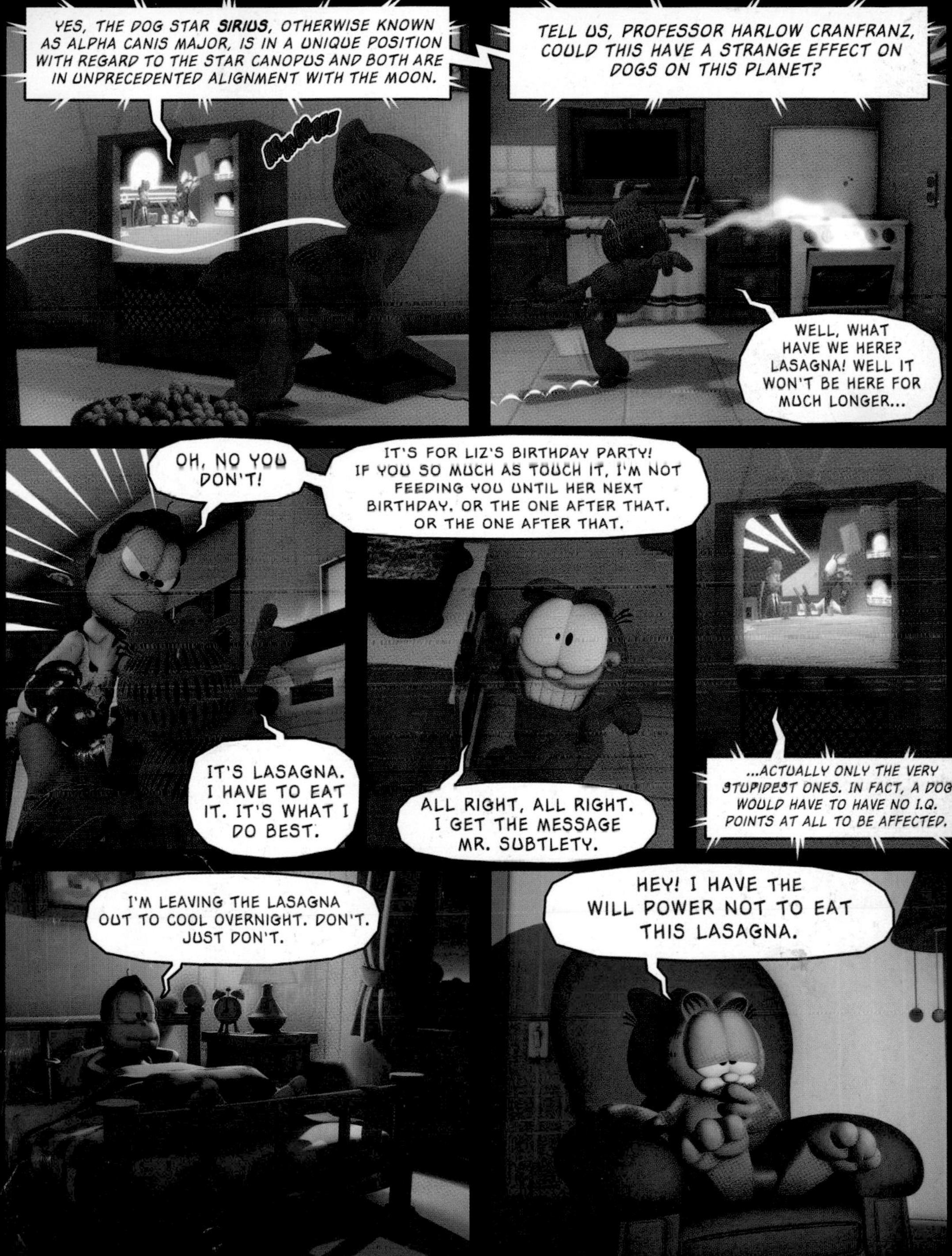
YES, THE DOG STAR SIRIUS, OTHERWISE KNOWN AS ALPHA CANIS MAJOR, IS IN A UNIQUE POSITION WITH REGARD TO THE STAR CANOPUS AND BOTH ARE IN UNPRECEDENTED ALIGNMENT WITH THE MOON.
TELL US, PROFESSOR HARLOW CRANFRANZ, COULD THIS HAVE A STRANGE EFFECT ON DOGS ON THIS PLANET?
WELL, WHAT HAVE WE HERE? LASAGNA! WELL IT WON'T BE HERE FOR MUCH LONGER...
OH, NO YOU DON'T!
IT'S FOR LIZ'S BIRTHDAY PARTY! IF YOU SO MUCH AS TOUCH IT, I'M NOT FEEDING YOU UNTIL HER NEXT BIRTHDAY. OR THE ONE AFTER THAT. OR THE ONE AFTER THAT.
IT'S LASAGNA. I HAVE TO EAT IT. IT'S WHAT I DO BEST.
ALL RIGHT, ALL RIGHT. I GET THE MESSAGE MR. SUBTLETY.
...ACTUALLY ONLY THE VERY STUPIDEST ONES. IN FACT, A DOG WOULD HAVE TO HAVE NO I.Q. POINTS AT ALL TO BE AFFECTED.
I'M LEAVING THE LASAGNA OUT TO COOL OVERNIGHT. DON'T. JUST DON'T.
HEY! I HAVE THE WILL POWER NOT TO EAT THIS LASAGNA.

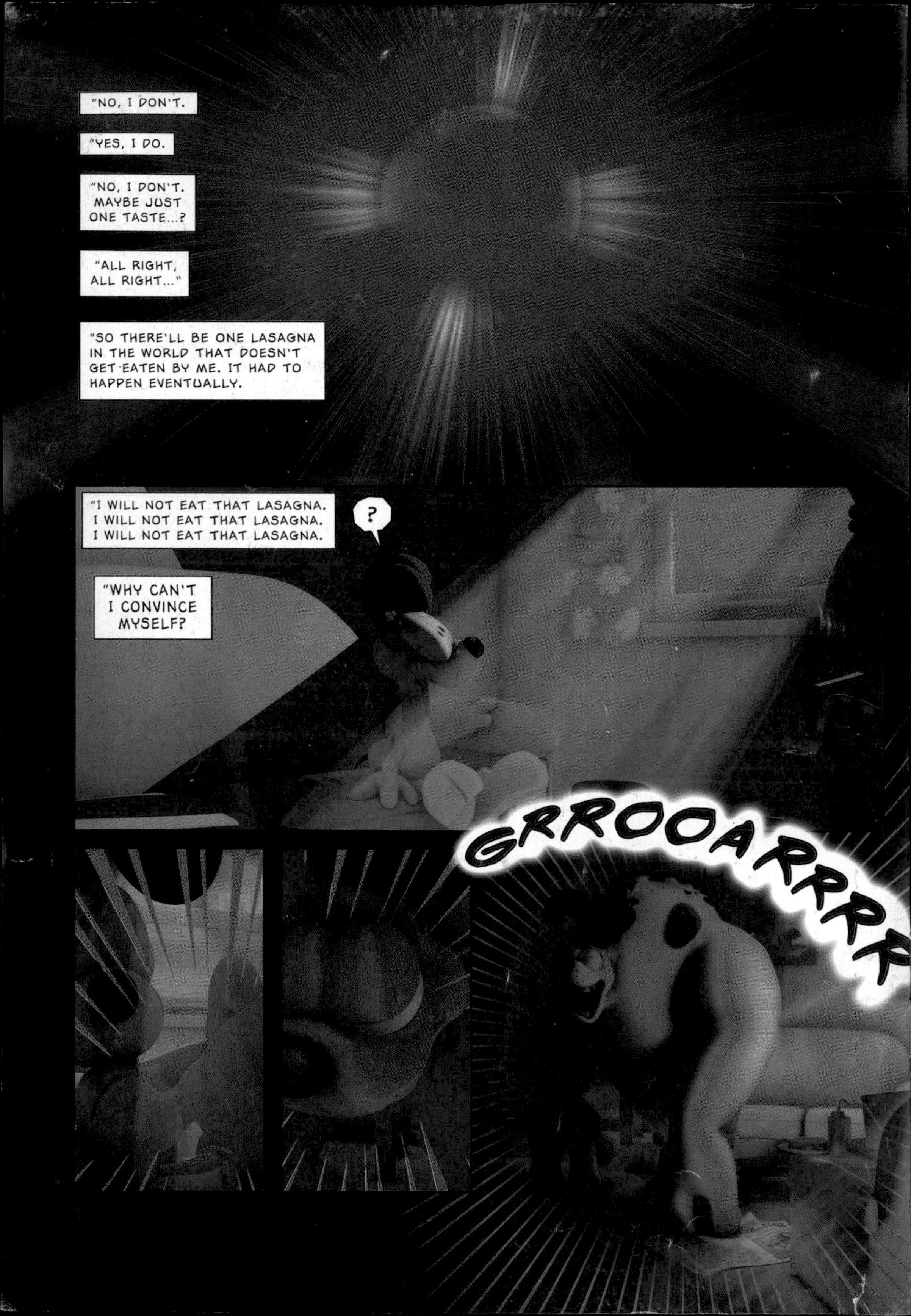
"NO, I DON'T.
"YES, I DO.
"NO, I DON'T. MAYBE JUST ONE TASTE...?
"ALL RIGHT, ALL RIGHT..."
"SO THERE'LL BE ONE LASAGNA IN THE WORLD THAT DOESN'T GET EATEN BY ME. IT HAD TO HAPPEN EVENTUALLY.
"I WILL NOT EAT THAT LASAGNA. I WILL NOT EAT THAT LASAGNA. I WILL NOT EAT THAT LASAGNA.
?
"WHY CAN'T I CONVINCE MYSELF?
GRROOARRRR

"I DON'T CARE HOW MUCH MY STOMACH GROWLS. I'M NOT GOING TO EAT THAT LASAGNA."

MMMM
MUNCH
CRUNCH

BANG
BOMB

EUH... WHAT'S THAT?

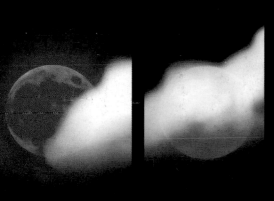

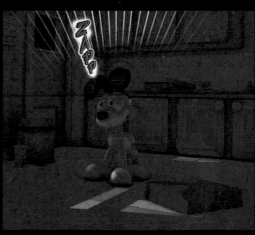

ZAPP

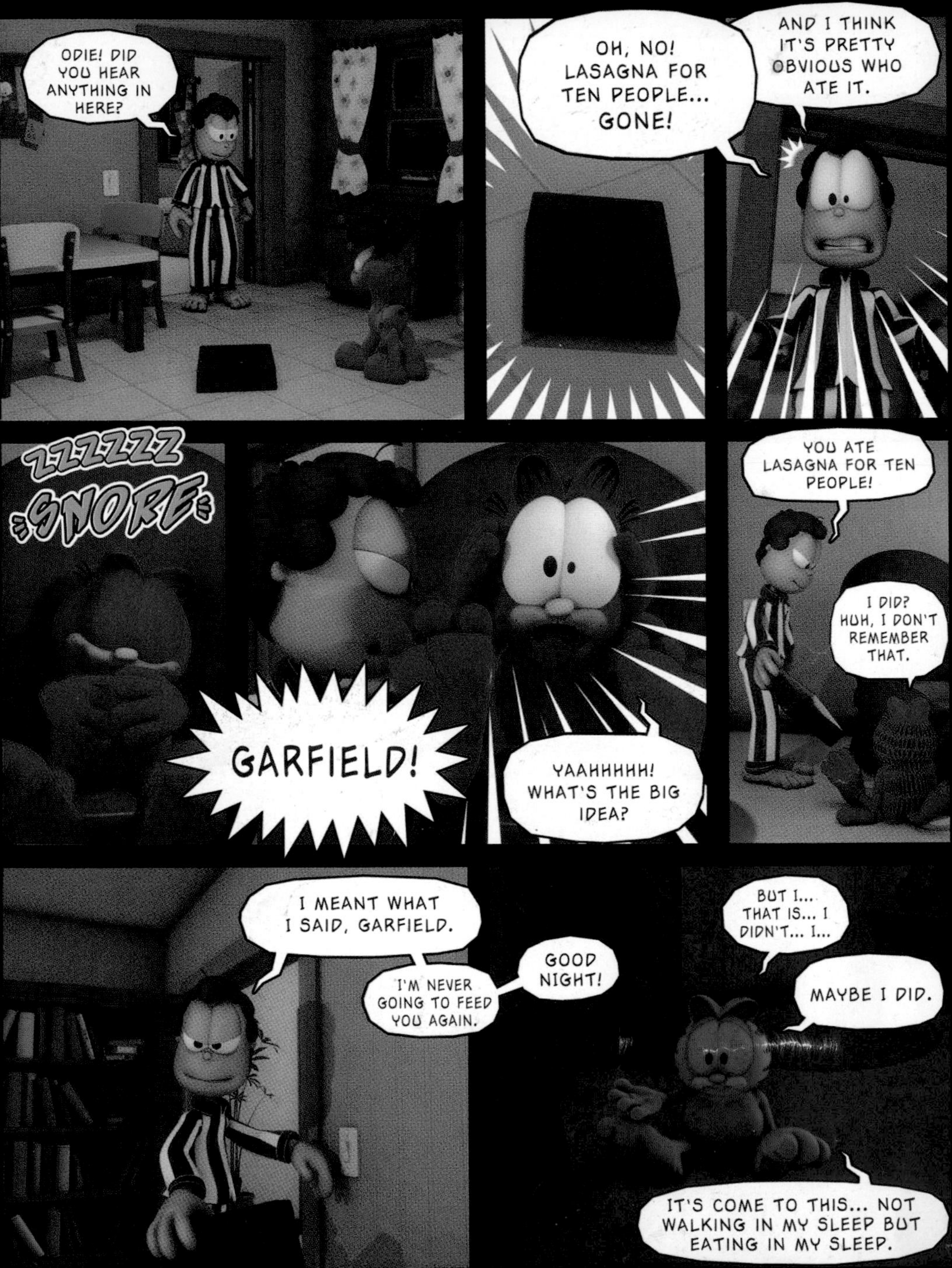

ODIE! DID YOU HEAR ANYTHING IN HERE?
OH, NO! LASAGNA FOR TEN PEOPLE... GONE!
AND I THINK IT'S PRETTY OBVIOUS WHO ATE IT.
ZZZZZZ
SNORE
GARFIELD!
YAAHHHHH! WHAT'S THE BIG IDEA?
YOU ATE LASAGNA FOR TEN PEOPLE!
I DID? HUH, I DON'T REMEMBER THAT.
I MEANT WHAT I SAID, GARFIELD.
I'M NEVER GOING TO FEED YOU AGAIN.
GOOD NIGHT!
BUT I... THAT IS... I DIDN'T... I...
MAYBE I DID.
IT'S COME TO THIS... NOT WALKING IN MY SLEEP BUT EATING IN MY SLEEP.

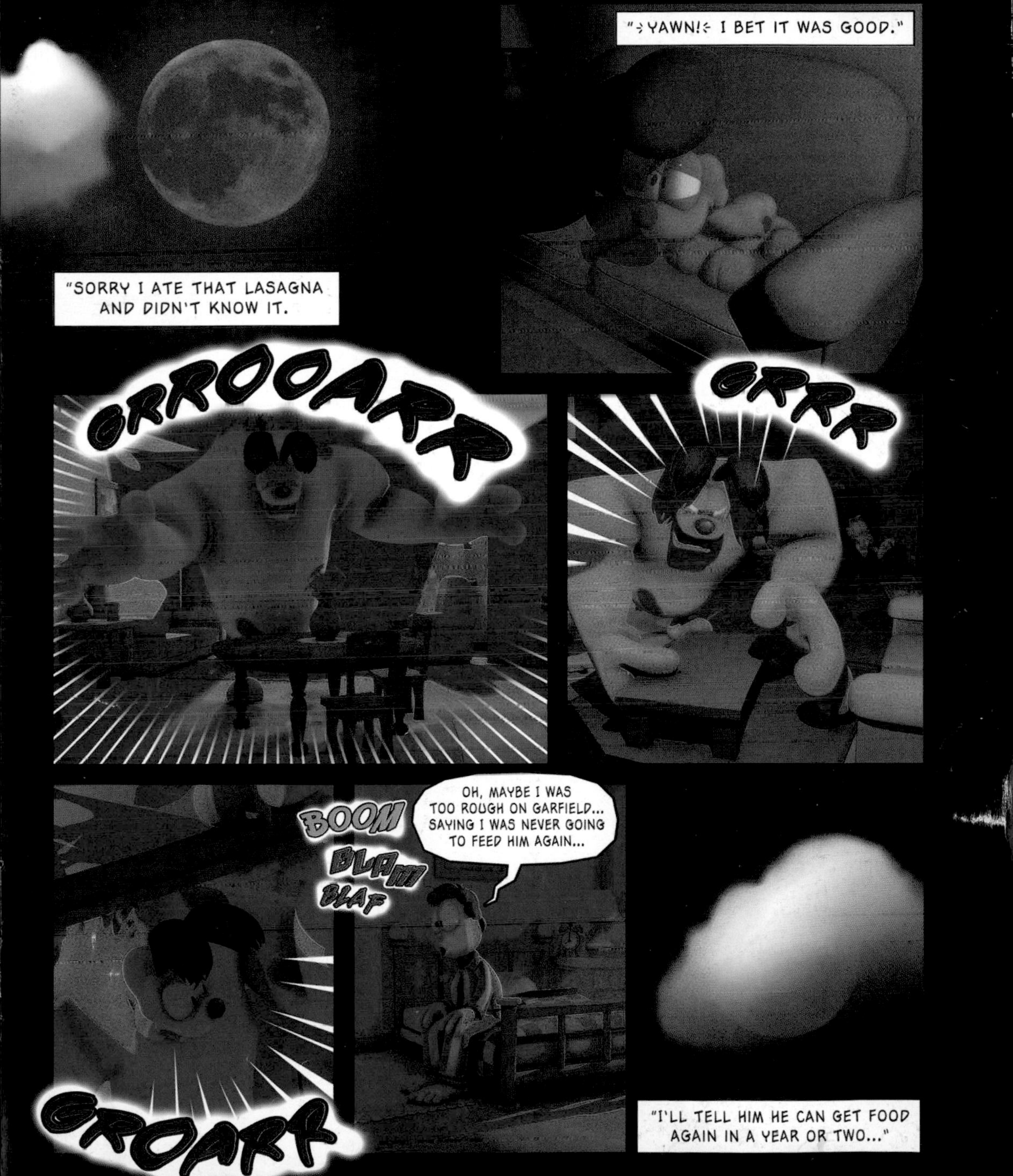
"SORRY I ATE THAT LASAGNA AND DIDN'T KNOW IT.
"YAWN! I BET IT WAS GOOD."
GRROOARR
GRRR
GROARR
BOOM
BLAM
BLAF
OH, MAYBE I WAS TOO ROUGH ON GARFIELD... SAYING I WAS NEVER GOING TO FEED HIM AGAIN...
"I'LL TELL HIM HE CAN GET FOOD AGAIN IN A YEAR OR TWO..."

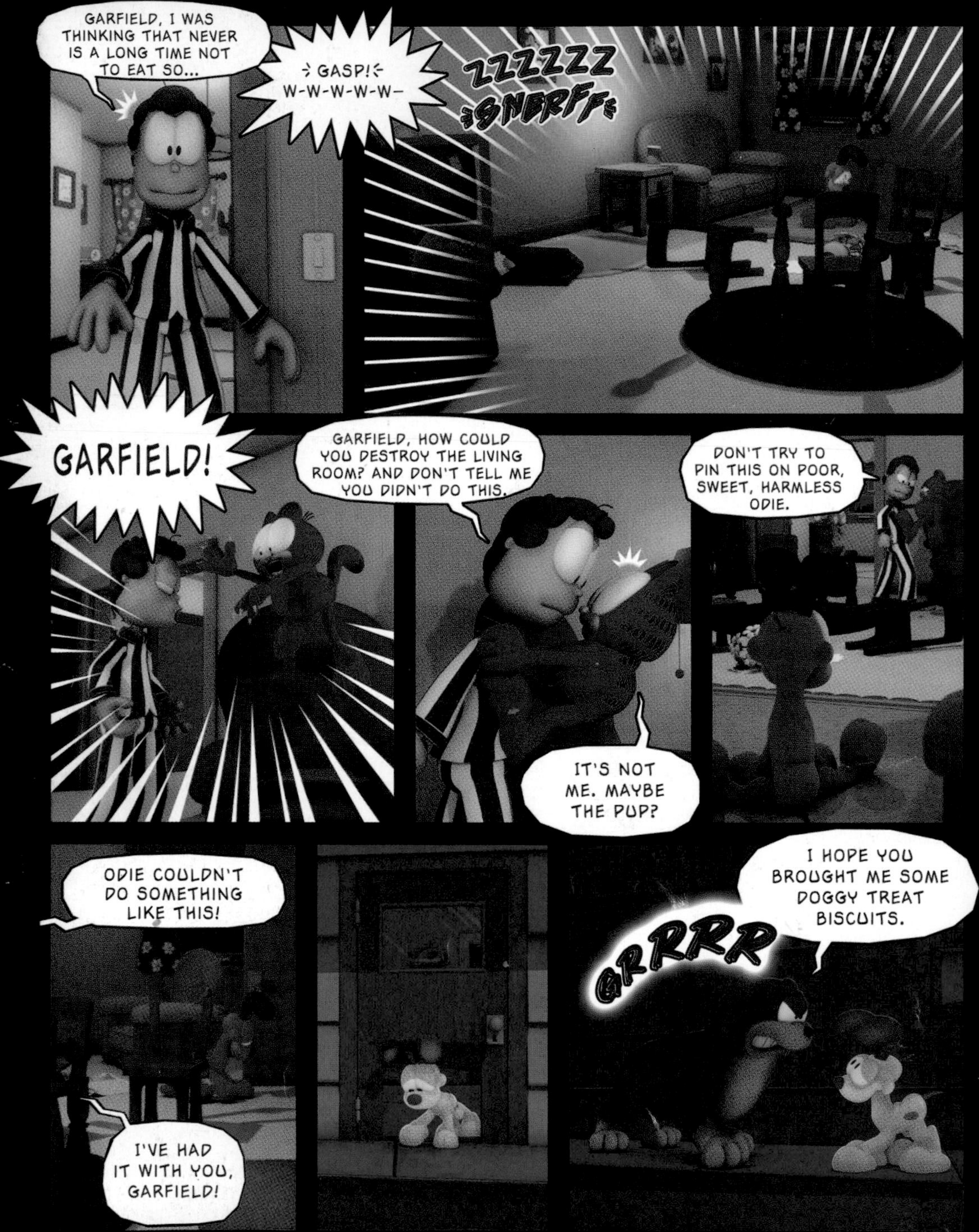
GARFIELD, I WAS THINKING THAT NEVER IS A LONG TIME NOT TO EAT SO...
GASP! W-W-W-W-W–
ZZZZZZ
SNERFF
GARFIELD!
GARFIELD, HOW COULD YOU DESTROY THE LIVING ROOM? AND DON'T TELL ME YOU DIDN'T DO THIS.
IT'S NOT ME. MAYBE THE PUP?
DON'T TRY TO PIN THIS ON POOR, SWEET, HARMLESS ODIE.
ODIE COULDN'T DO SOMETHING LIKE THIS!
I'VE HAD IT WITH YOU, GARFIELD!
I HOPE YOU BROUGHT ME SOME DOGGY TREAT BISCUITS.
GRRRR

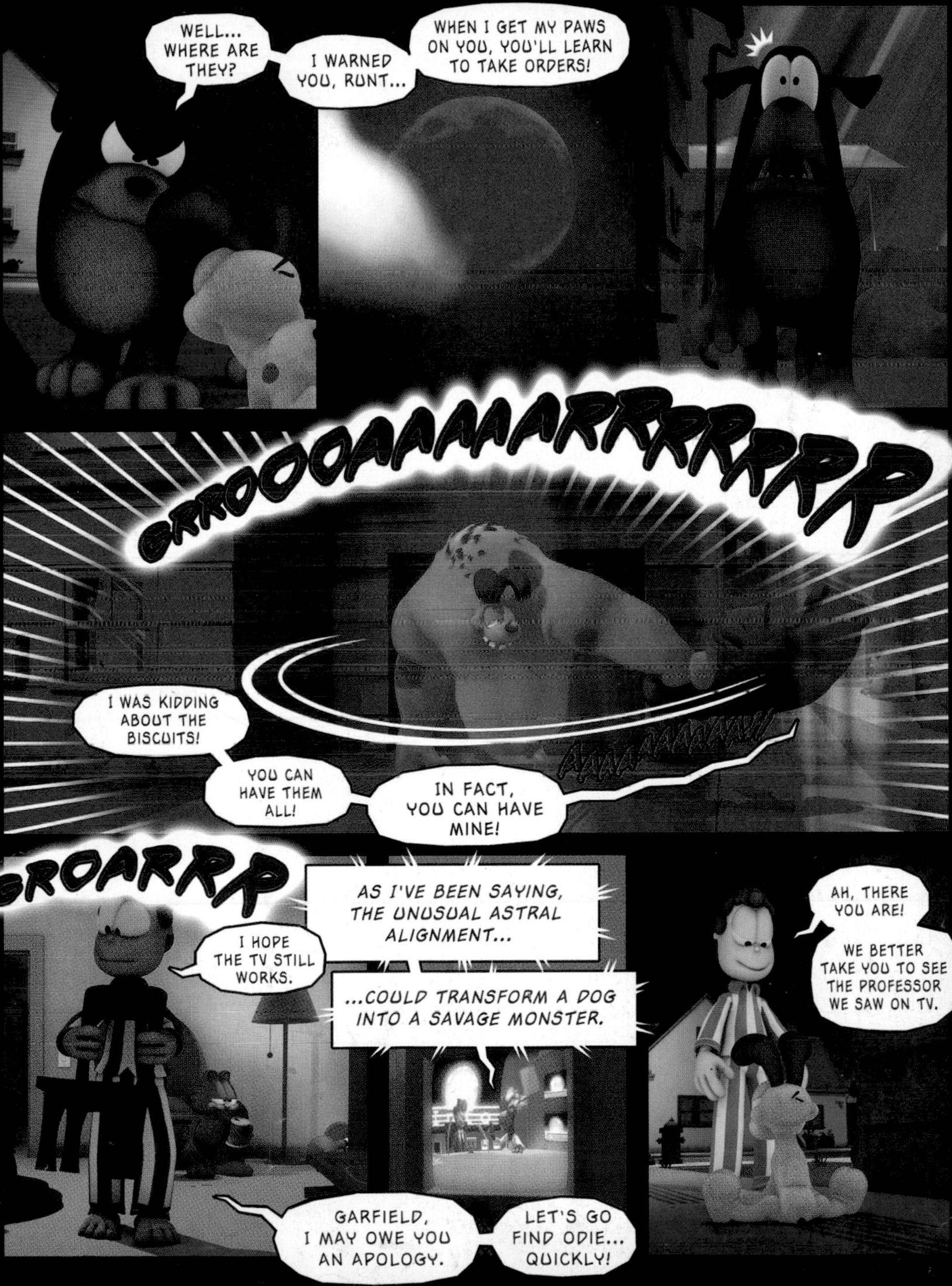

WELL... WHERE ARE THEY?
I WARNED YOU, RUNT...
WHEN I GET MY PAWS ON YOU, YOU'LL LEARN TO TAKE ORDERS!
GRROOOOAAAAAARRRRRRRR
I WAS KIDDING ABOUT THE BISCUITS!
YOU CAN HAVE THEM ALL!
IN FACT, YOU CAN HAVE MINE!
GROARRR
I HOPE THE TV STILL WORKS.
AS I'VE BEEN SAYING, THE UNUSUAL ASTRAL ALIGNMENT...
...COULD TRANSFORM A DOG INTO A SAVAGE MONSTER.
GARFIELD, I MAY OWE YOU AN APOLOGY.
LET'S GO FIND ODIE... QUICKLY!
AH, THERE YOU ARE!
WE BETTER TAKE YOU TO SEE THE PROFESSOR WE SAW ON TV.

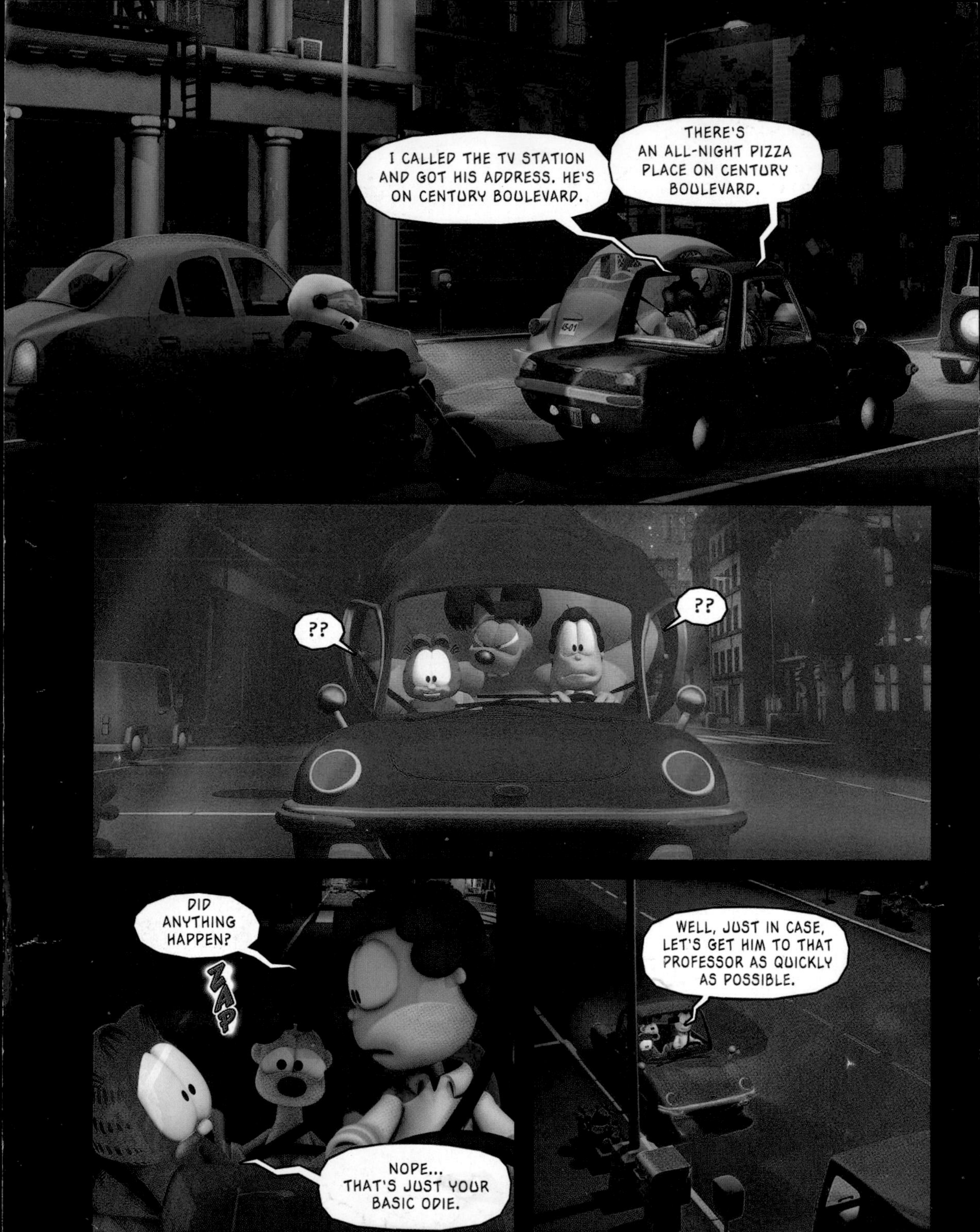
I CALLED THE TV STATION AND GOT HIS ADDRESS. HE'S ON CENTURY BOULEVARD.
THERE'S AN ALL-NIGHT PIZZA PLACE ON CENTURY BOULEVARD.
??
??
DID ANYTHING HAPPEN?
ZAP
NOPE... THAT'S JUST YOUR BASIC ODIE.
WELL, JUST IN CASE, LET'S GET HIM TO THAT PROFESSOR AS QUICKLY AS POSSIBLE.

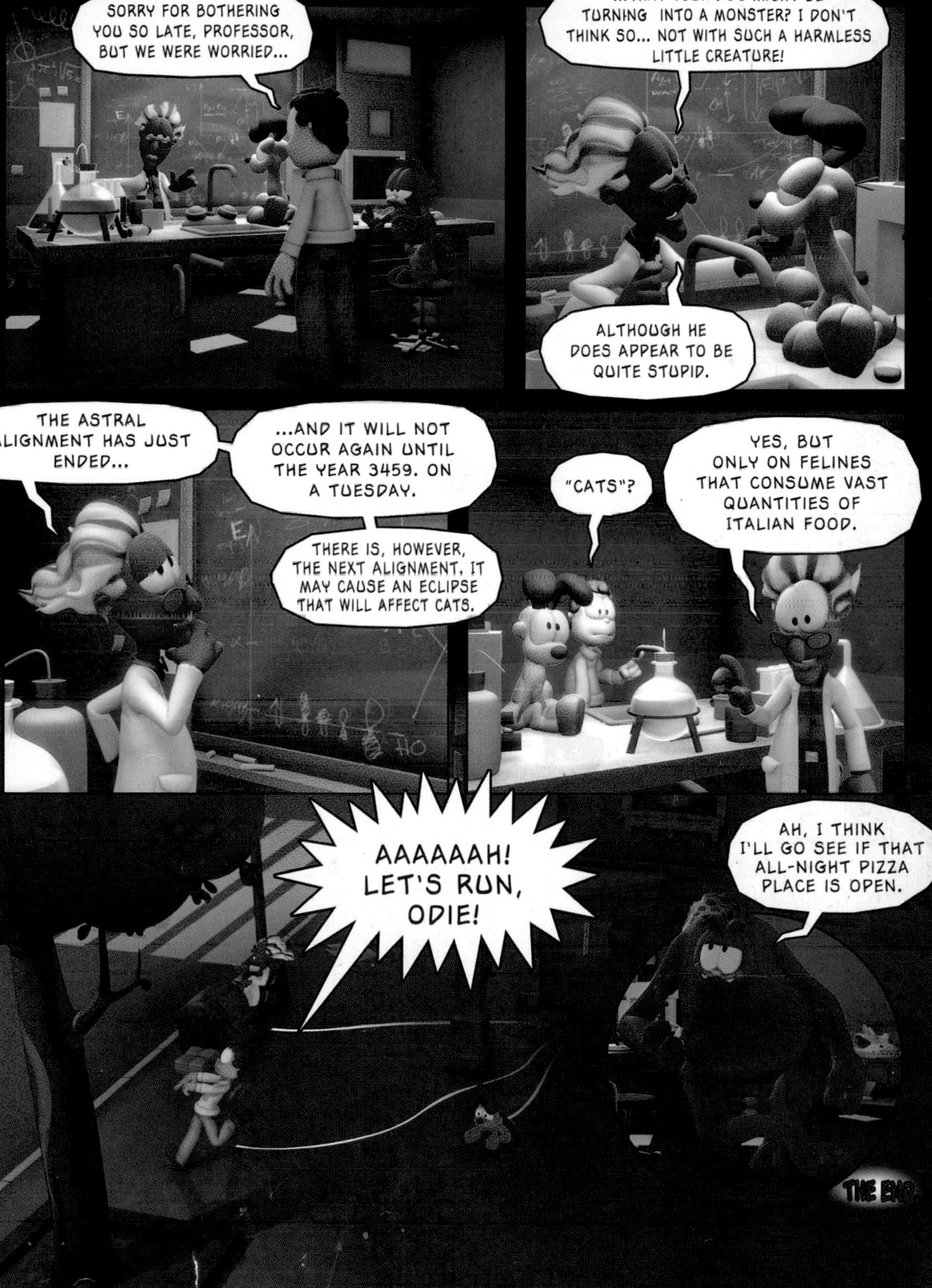
SORRY FOR BOTHERING YOU SO LATE, PROFESSOR, BUT WE WERE WORRIED...
...THAT YOUR DOG MIGHT BE TURNING INTO A MONSTER? I DON'T THINK SO... NOT WITH SUCH A HARMLESS LITTLE CREATURE!
ALTHOUGH HE DOES APPEAR TO BE QUITE STUPID.
THE ASTRAL ALIGNMENT HAS JUST ENDED...
...AND IT WILL NOT OCCUR AGAIN UNTIL THE YEAR 3459. ON A TUESDAY.
THERE IS, HOWEVER, THE NEXT ALIGNMENT. IT MAY CAUSE AN ECLIPSE THAT WILL AFFECT CATS.
"CATS"?
YES, BUT ONLY ON FELINES THAT CONSUME VAST QUANTITIES OF ITALIAN FOOD.
AAAAAAH! LET'S RUN, ODIE!
AH, I THINK I'LL GO SEE IF THAT ALL-NIGHT PIZZA PLACE IS OPEN.
THE END

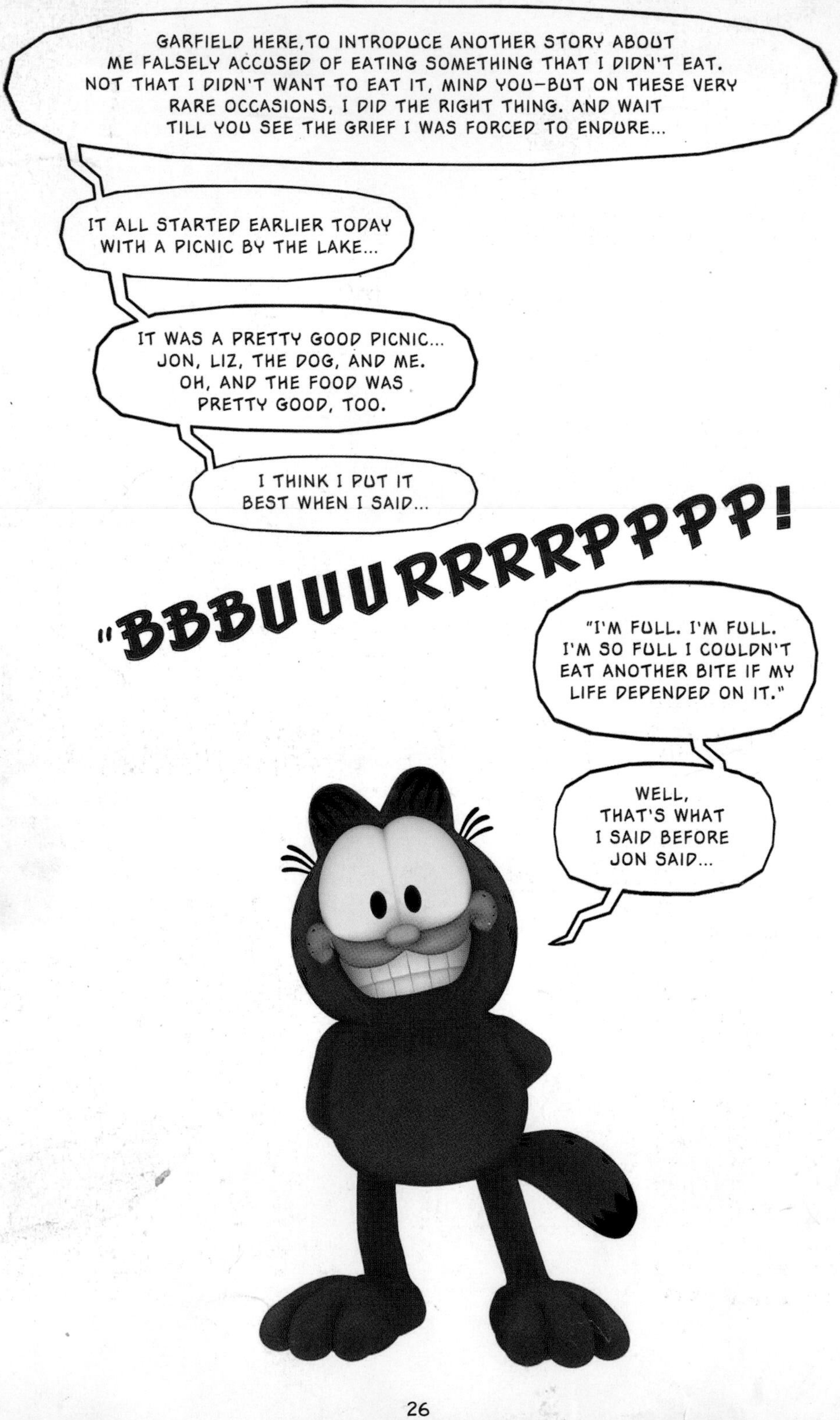
GARFIELD HERE,TO INTRODUCE ANOTHER STORY ABOUT ME FALSELY ACCUSED OF EATING SOMETHING THAT I DIDN'T EAT. NOT THAT I DIDN'T WANT TO EAT IT, MIND YOU—BUT ON THESE VERY RARE OCCASIONS, I DID THE RIGHT THING. AND WAIT TILL YOU SEE THE GRIEF I WAS FORCED TO ENDURE...
IT ALL STARTED EARLIER TODAY WITH A PICNIC BY THE LAKE...
IT WAS A PRETTY GOOD PICNIC... JON, LIZ, THE DOG, AND ME. OH, AND THE FOOD WAS PRETTY GOOD, TOO.
I THINK I PUT IT BEST WHEN I SAID...
"BBBUUURRRRPPPPP!
"I'M FULL. I'M FULL. I'M SO FULL I COULDN'T EAT ANOTHER BITE IF MY LIFE DEPENDED ON IT."
WELL, THAT'S WHAT I SAID BEFORE JON SAID...

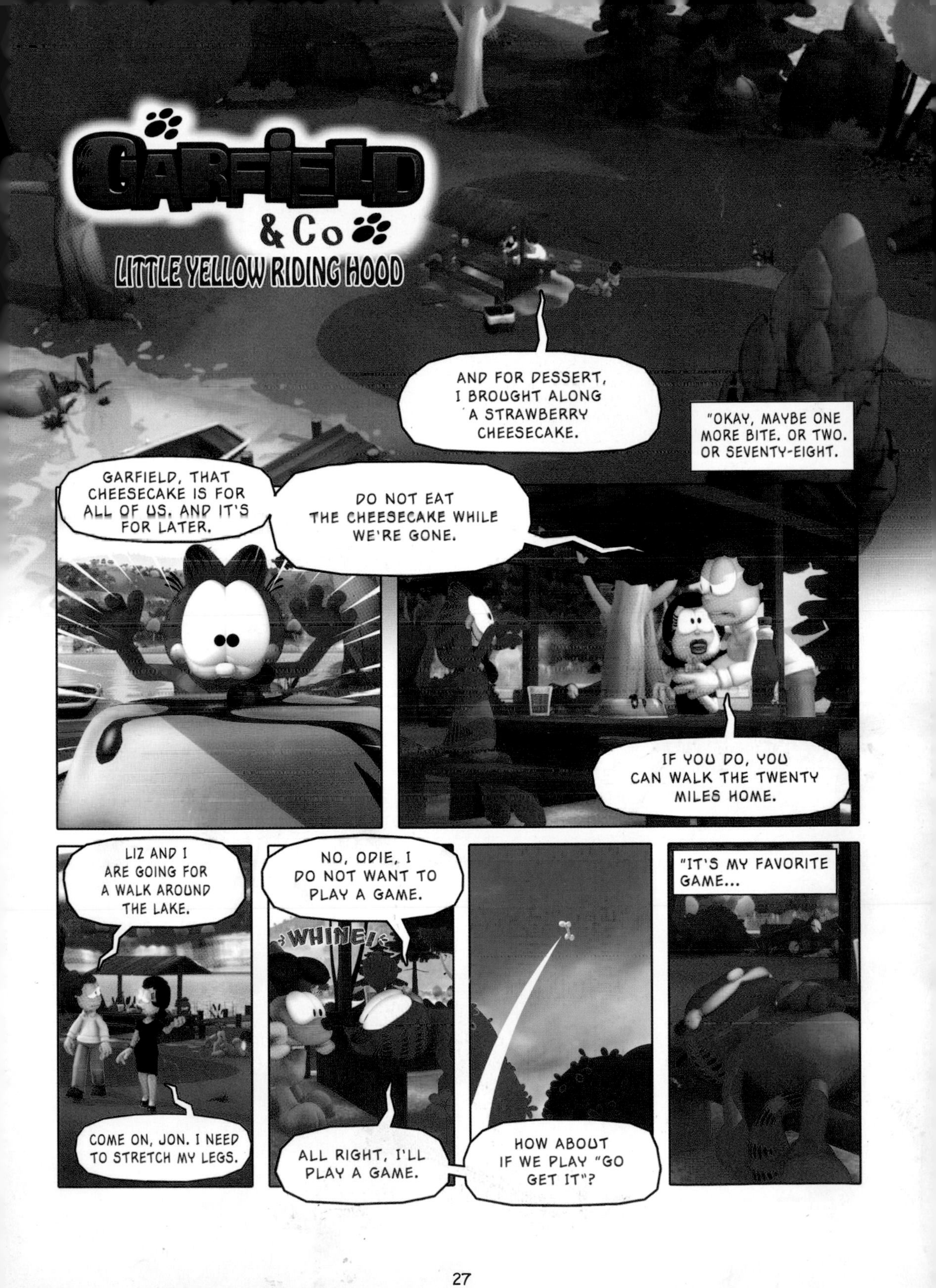
GARFIELD
& Co
LITTLE YELLOW RIDING HOOD
AND FOR DESSERT, I BROUGHT ALONG A STRAWBERRY CHEESECAKE.
"OKAY, MAYBE ONE MORE BITE. OR TWO. OR SEVENTY-EIGHT.
GARFIELD, THAT CHEESECAKE IS FOR ALL OF US. AND IT'S FOR LATER.
DO NOT EAT THE CHEESECAKE WHILE WE'RE GONE.
IF YOU DO, YOU CAN WALK THE TWENTY MILES HOME.
LIZ AND I ARE GOING FOR A WALK AROUND THE LAKE.
COME ON, JON. I NEED TO STRETCH MY LEGS.
NO, ODIE, I DO NOT WANT TO PLAY A GAME.
WHINE!
ALL RIGHT, I'LL PLAY A GAME.
HOW ABOUT IF WE PLAY "GO GET IT"?
"IT'S MY FAVORITE GAME...

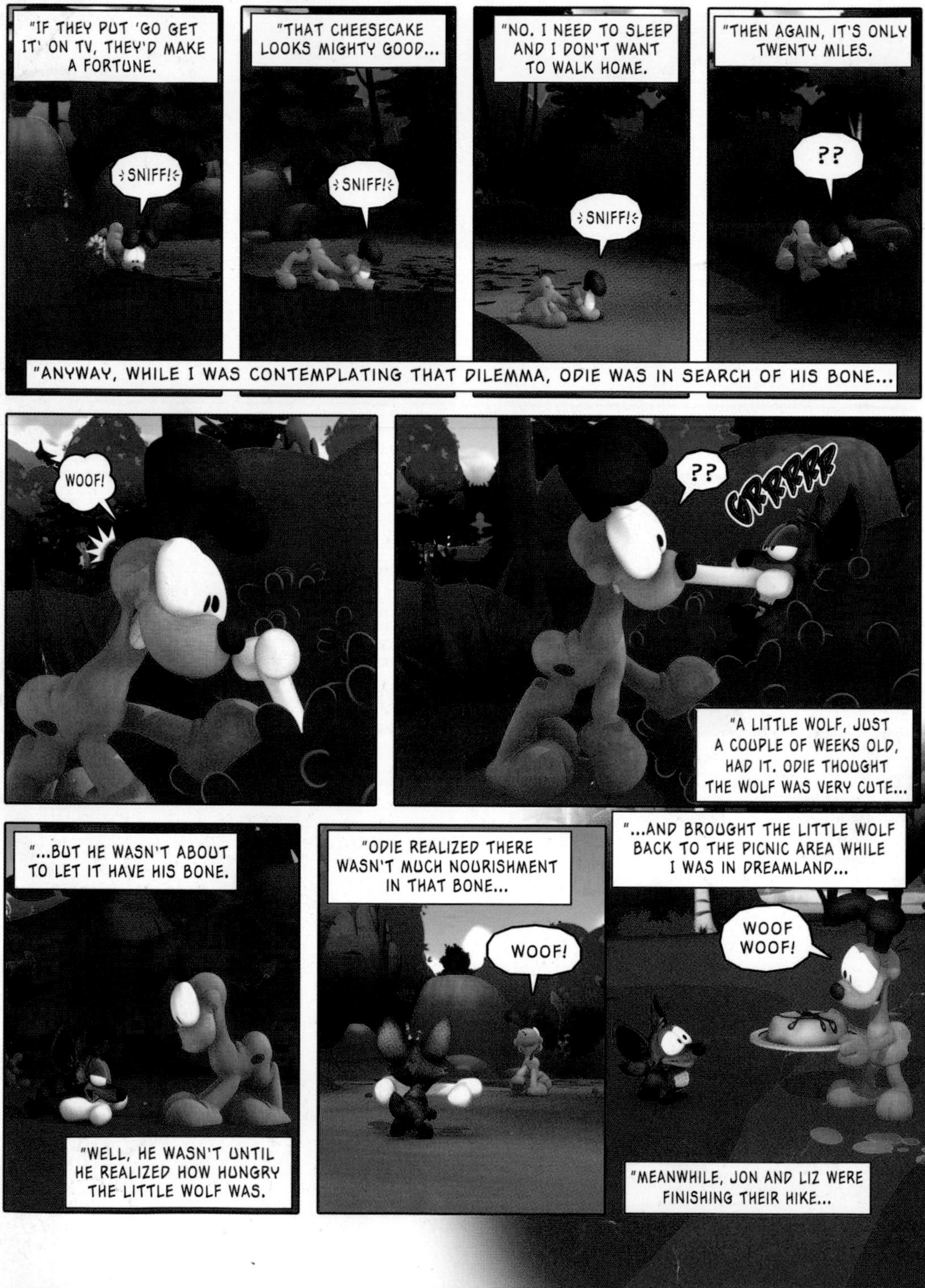
"IF THEY PUT 'GO GET IT' ON TV, THEY'D MAKE A FORTUNE.
SNIFF!
"THAT CHEESECAKE LOOKS MIGHTY GOOD...
SNIFF!
"NO. I NEED TO SLEEP AND I DON'T WANT TO WALK HOME.
SNIFF!
"THEN AGAIN, IT'S ONLY TWENTY MILES.
??
"ANYWAY, WHILE I WAS CONTEMPLATING THAT DILEMMA, ODIE WAS IN SEARCH OF HIS BONE...
WOOF!
??
GRRRRR
"A LITTLE WOLF, JUST A COUPLE OF WEEKS OLD, HAD IT. ODIE THOUGHT THE WOLF WAS VERY CUTE...
"...BUT HE WASN'T ABOUT TO LET IT HAVE HIS BONE.
"WELL, HE WASN'T UNTIL HE REALIZED HOW HUNGRY THE LITTLE WOLF WAS.
"ODIE REALIZED THERE WASN'T MUCH NOURISHMENT IN THAT BONE...
WOOF!
"...AND BROUGHT THE LITTLE WOLF BACK TO THE PICNIC AREA WHILE I WAS IN DREAMLAND...
WOOF WOOF!
"MEANWHILE, JON AND LIZ WERE FINISHING THEIR HIKE...

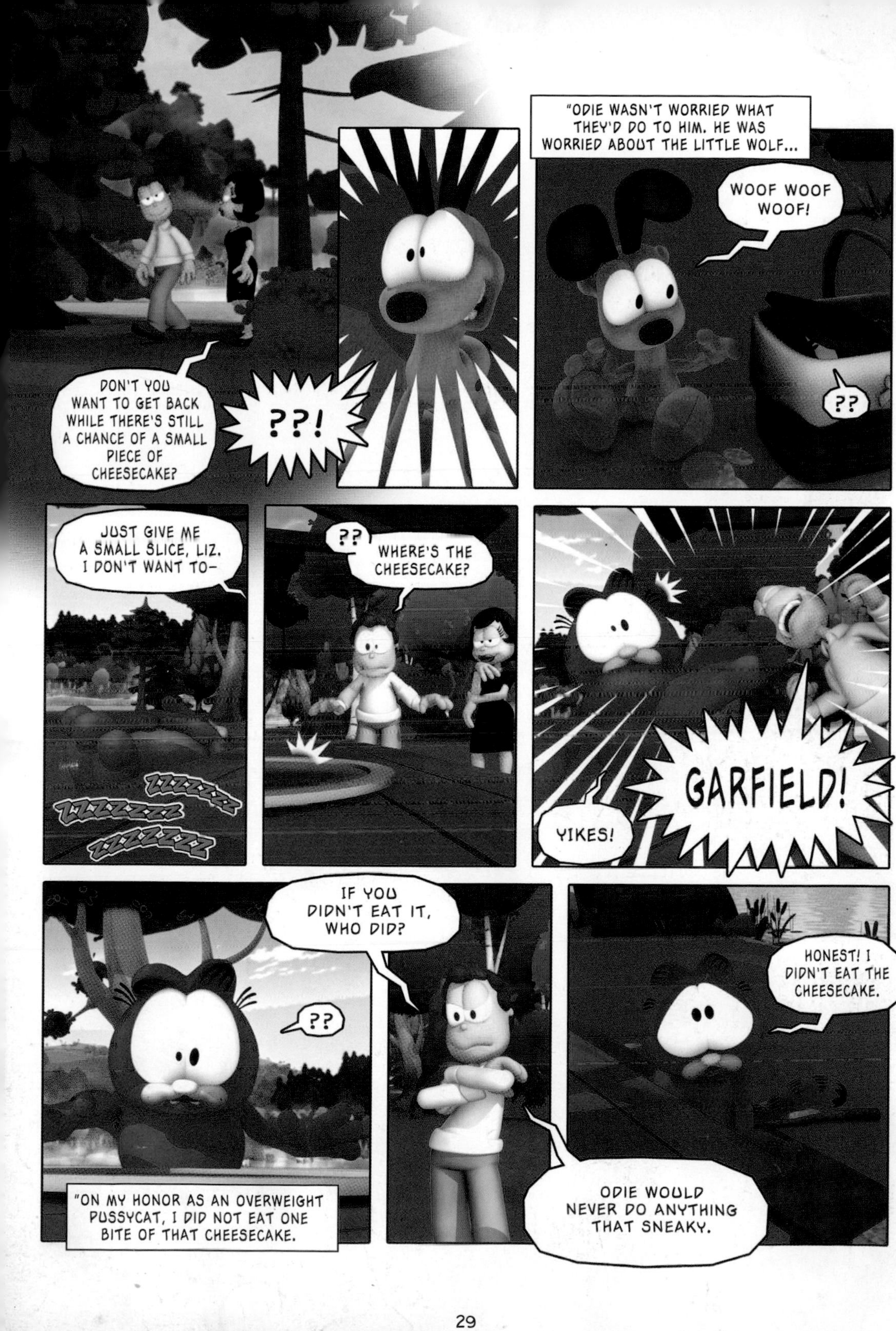
DON'T YOU WANT TO GET BACK WHILE THERE'S STILL A CHANCE OF A SMALL PIECE OF CHEESECAKE?
??!
"ODIE WASN'T WORRIED WHAT THEY'D DO TO HIM. HE WAS WORRIED ABOUT THE LITTLE WOLF...
WOOF WOOF WOOF!
??
JUST GIVE ME A SMALL SLICE, LIZ. I DON'T WANT TO-
ZZZZZZZZ
??
WHERE'S THE CHEESECAKE?
GARFIELD!
YIKES!
IF YOU DIDN'T EAT IT, WHO DID?
??
"ON MY HONOR AS AN OVERWEIGHT PUSSYCAT, I DID NOT EAT ONE BITE OF THAT CHEESECAKE.
ODIE WOULD NEVER DO ANYTHING THAT SNEAKY.
HONEST! I DIDN'T EAT THE CHEESECAKE.

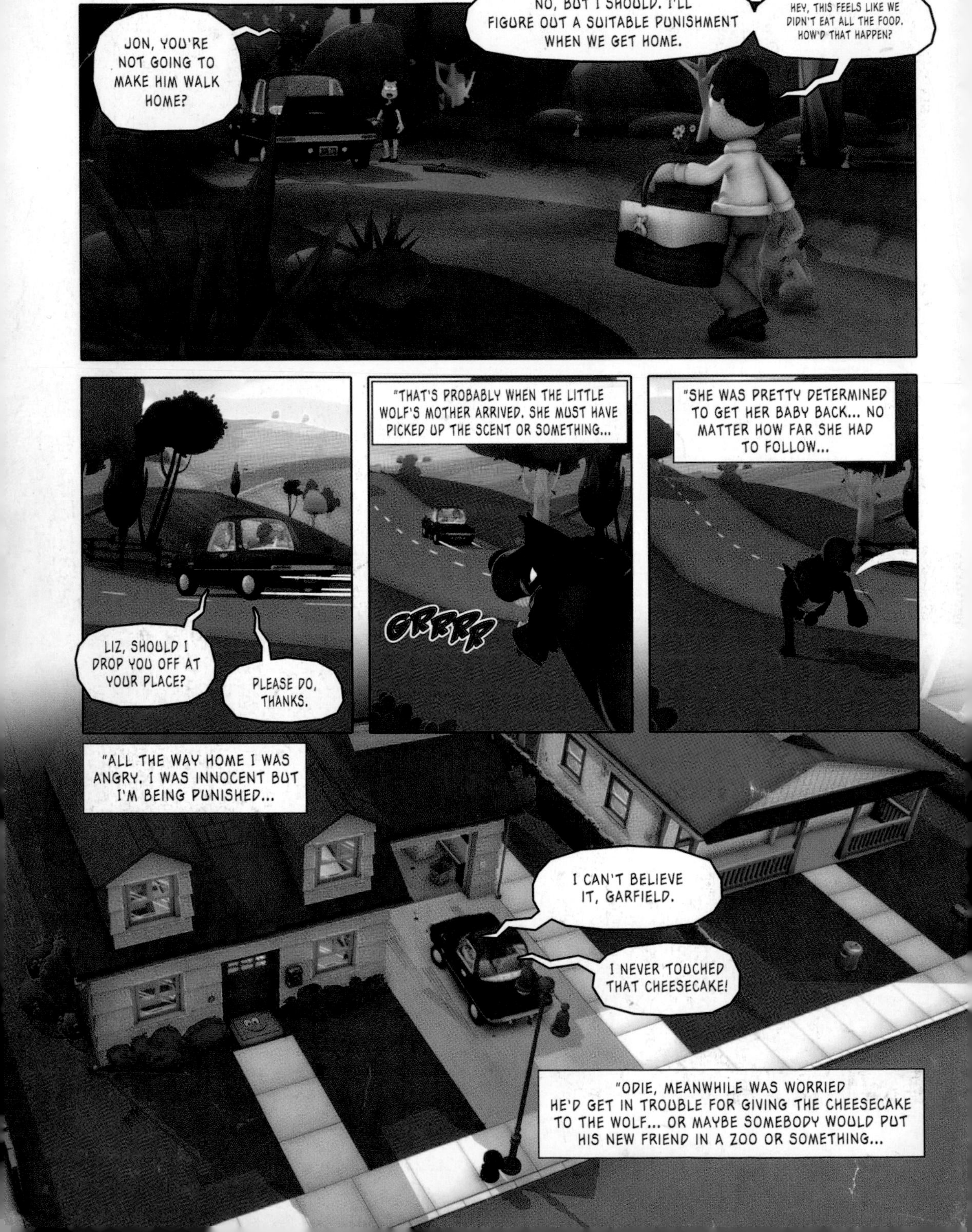
JON, YOU'RE NOT GOING TO MAKE HIM WALK HOME?
NO, BUT I SHOULD. I'LL FIGURE OUT A SUITABLE PUNISHMENT WHEN WE GET HOME.
HEY, THIS FEELS LIKE WE DIDN'T EAT ALL THE FOOD. HOW'D THAT HAPPEN?
LIZ, SHOULD I DROP YOU OFF AT YOUR PLACE?
PLEASE DO, THANKS.
"THAT'S PROBABLY WHEN THE LITTLE WOLF'S MOTHER ARRIVED. SHE MUST HAVE PICKED UP THE SCENT OR SOMETHING...
GRRRR
"SHE WAS PRETTY DETERMINED TO GET HER BABY BACK... NO MATTER HOW FAR SHE HAD TO FOLLOW...
"ALL THE WAY HOME I WAS ANGRY. I WAS INNOCENT BUT I'M BEING PUNISHED...
I CAN'T BELIEVE IT, GARFIELD.
I NEVER TOUCHED THAT CHEESECAKE!
"ODIE, MEANWHILE WAS WORRIED HE'D GET IN TROUBLE FOR GIVING THE CHEESECAKE TO THE WOLF... OR MAYBE SOMEBODY WOULD PUT HIS NEW FRIEND IN A ZOO OR SOMETHING...

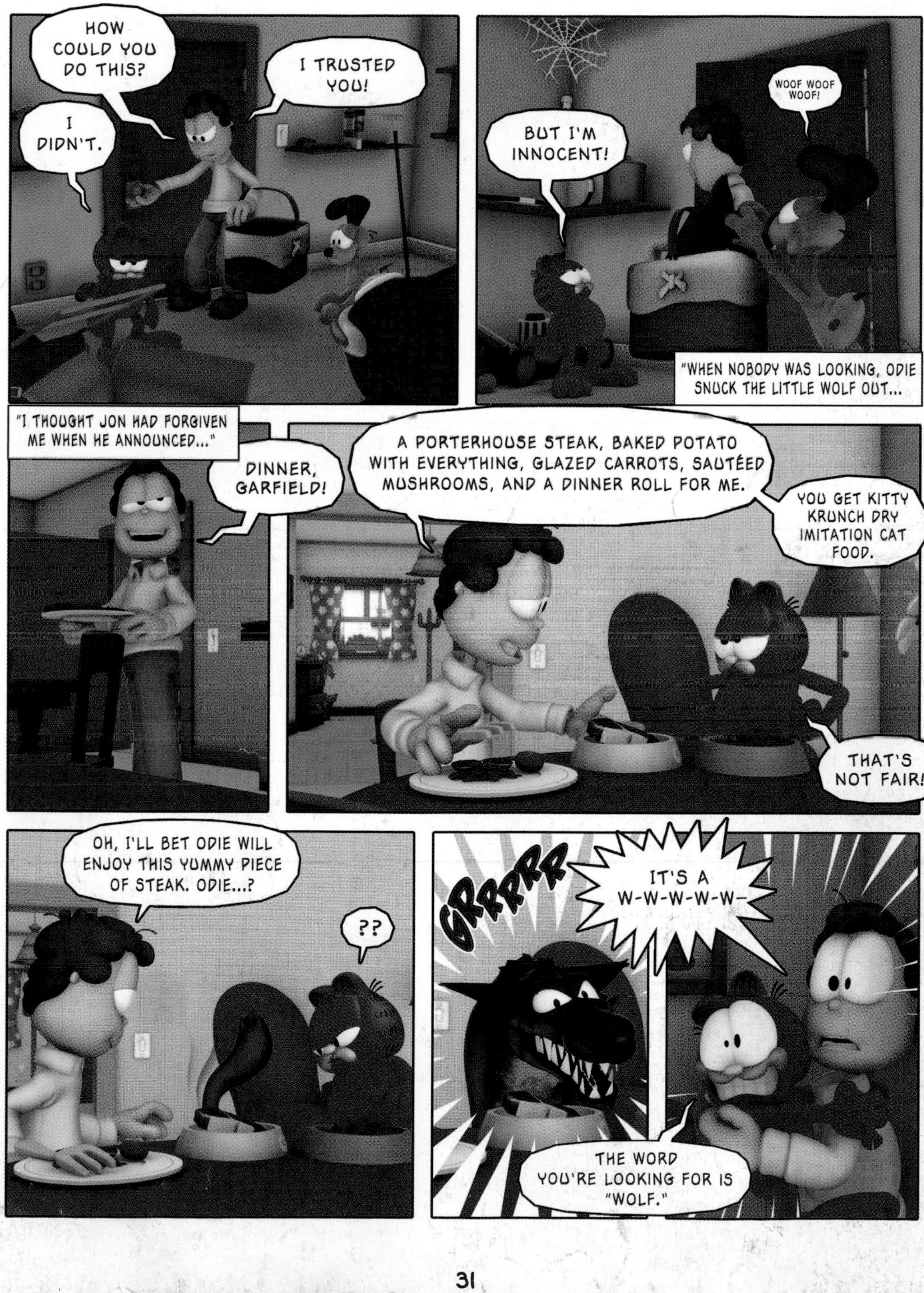

HOW COULD YOU DO THIS?
I TRUSTED YOU!
I DIDN'T.
WOOF WOOF WOOF!
BUT I'M INNOCENT!
"WHEN NOBODY WAS LOOKING, ODIE SNUCK THE LITTLE WOLF OUT...
"I THOUGHT JON HAD FORGIVEN ME WHEN HE ANNOUNCED..."
DINNER, GARFIELD!
A PORTERHOUSE STEAK, BAKED POTATO WITH EVERYTHING, GLAZED CARROTS, SAUTÉED MUSHROOMS, AND A DINNER ROLL FOR ME.
YOU GET KITTY KRUNCH DRY IMITATION CAT FOOD.
THAT'S NOT FAIR!
OH, I'LL BET ODIE WILL ENJOY THIS YUMMY PIECE OF STEAK. ODIE...?
??
GRRRRR
IT'S A W-W-W-W-W–
THE WORD YOU'RE LOOKING FOR IS "WOLF."

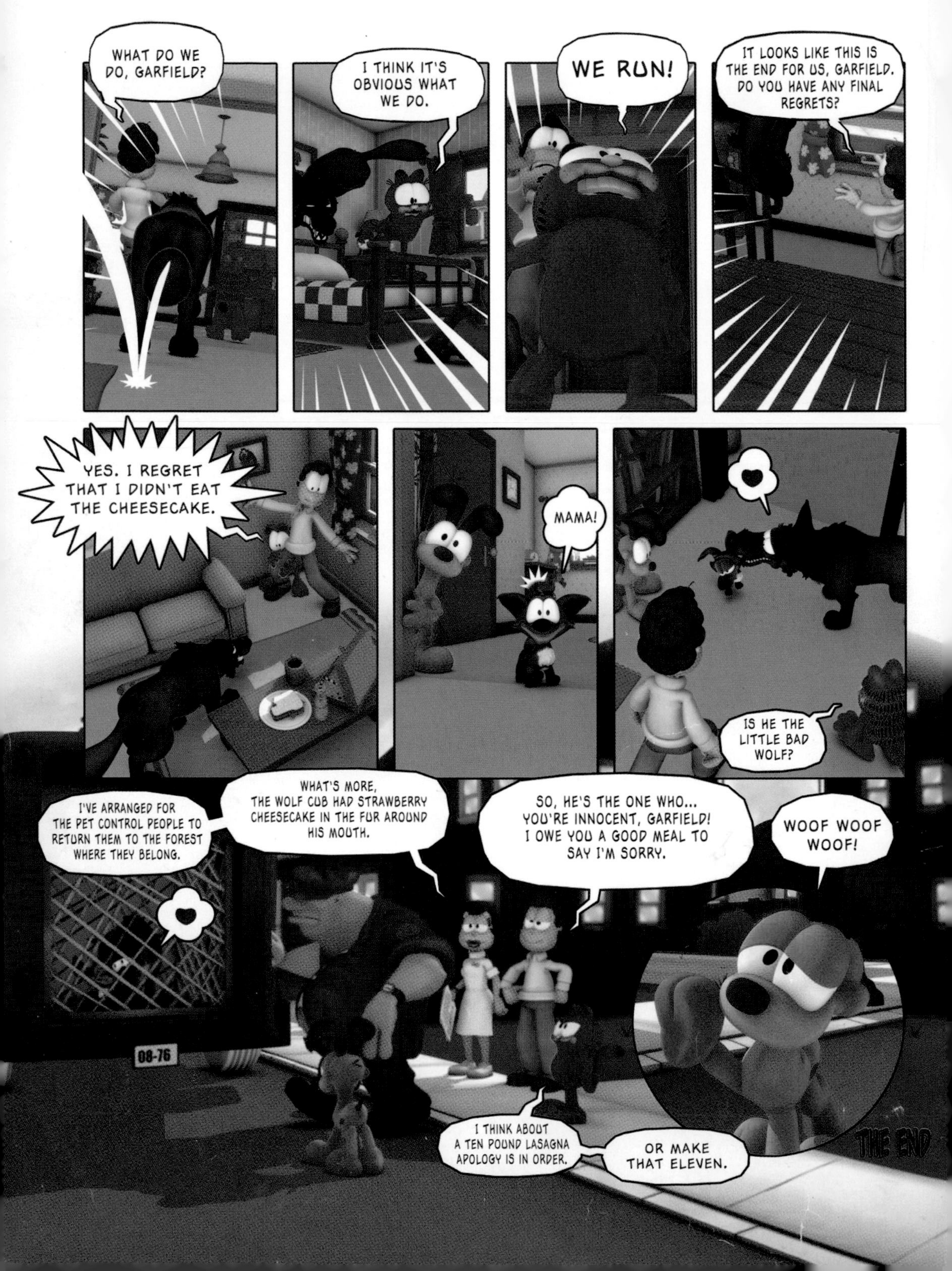

WHAT DO WE DO, GARFIELD?
I THINK IT'S OBVIOUS WHAT WE DO.
WE RUN!
IT LOOKS LIKE THIS IS THE END FOR US, GARFIELD. DO YOU HAVE ANY FINAL REGRETS?
YES. I REGRET THAT I DIDN'T EAT THE CHEESECAKE.
MAMA!
IS HE THE LITTLE BAD WOLF?
I'VE ARRANGED FOR THE PET CONTROL PEOPLE TO RETURN THEM TO THE FOREST WHERE THEY BELONG.
WHAT'S MORE, THE WOLF CUB HAD STRAWBERRY CHEESECAKE IN THE FUR AROUND HIS MOUTH.
SO, HE'S THE ONE WHO... YOU'RE INNOCENT, GARFIELD! I OWE YOU A GOOD MEAL TO SAY I'M SORRY.
WOOF WOOF WOOF!
08-76
I THINK ABOUT A TEN POUND LASAGNA APOLOGY IS IN ORDER.
OR MAKE THAT ELEVEN.
THE END